The Art of The Deal
13¹/² Inches of Manhood

The Author Mr. De

The Art of The Deal
Copyright © 2021 by The Author Mr. De

All rights reserved. No part of this publication may be reproduced, distributed, or transmitted in any form or by any means, including photocopying, recording, or other electronic or mechanical methods, without the prior written permission of the publisher or author, except in the case of brief quotations embodied in critical reviews and certain other noncommercial uses permitted by copyright law.

Although every precaution has been taken to verify the accuracy of the information contained herein, the author and publisher assume no responsibility for any errors or omissions. No liability is assumed for damages that may result from the use of information contained within.

Library of Congress Control Number: 2021902425
ISBN-13: Paperback: 978-1-64749-348-6
          ePub: 978-1-64749-349-3

Printed in the United States of America

GoToPublish LLC
1-888-337-1724
www.gotopublish.com
info@gotopublish.com

It was 12 July early morning, 6:00 a.m., to be exact when I noticed a stunning hunk of a man arriving at a residence just across the street from me. I could hardly believe my eyes. A city cab driver was assisting him with his luggage as the gentleman stood there in an erect stance of military dominance. He counted out his fare and handed it to the driver. I was up early because I was unable to sleep for whatever reason. In some way, it really paid off. I was nothing less than mesmerized by the sight of such a fine human specimen. I was captivated in a trance while watching this man, as I peeped through the curtain. I tried reasoning in my mind, while totally captivated with amazement, How could any man be so perfectly built and adorned with so much sex appeal? In my estimation, he had to be at least six feet four with bulging muscles so defined you would have thought he was chiseled out of a rock. In fact, you would have thought he spent every passing moment working out in a gym with a very rigorous routine. He definitely had the body to prove it.

Interesting enough, it was challenging to believe what I was witnessing. Just by the mere fact I was only doing my morning routine, and lo and behold, I was able to capture quite vividly in my mind the most spectacular sight any woman would want to greet her so early in the morning. Believe me when I tell you words are not adequate for me to describe this most mind-blowing sight. All I could say was, Damn! Who is that nigga? I mean shit, I had to do a double, nawl, a triple look, totally in disbelief. I'm standing here at the window thinking, Who in the hell is this man? I was completely frozen in place as I watched every movement he made while gathering his luggage and other items just after the cab had driven away. Everything about this man was a damn phenomenon! His hair was mid-shoulder dreads. I could even see that his teeth were pearly white as he talked and laughed with the cab driver before he left. I began to wonder if he knew someone was watching him. He took a moment to place his luggage on the porch and turned slowly around facing the street where he began stretching in a horizontal stance, slowly inhaling and exhaling each breath. Taking his time to slowly bend over to touch his toes in a back and forth motion. Once he stood back in an upright position, he began flexing his arm muscles, and taking a few sitting squats. It was as if he was purposely putting on a show for whoever was watching.

Although 6:00 a.m. is early for most people, it was my daily routine to get up this time of morning and start my day. I could tell he was used to being up early as well. As I looked closer, I could see he had luggage that indicated he was a US Navy Serviceman. This would also explain his desire to maintain an exercise regimen to maintain his early morning energy boost.

I could see clearly, the driver insisted on helping this hunk of a man with his luggage; however, the man, who would later introduce himself to me as Styles, very kindly resisted. Soon after the cab driver left the residence, Styles began to place each item meticulously on the porch in a militarized formation. Once the last item was place on the porch. Styles began an exercise routine that would blow you away. It was as if he was engaged in a sexual suggestive stripping body posturing. I could not believe what I was seeing. After a brief moment of intense stretching and routines, he removed his shirt and I was like, damn this black ass man is fucking sexy as hell! It was like I was watching some Rated X kind of shit! I could not move! In fact, I did not move. As he continued to get more intense with his routines, I could see his large powerful muscles flexing like a tube filled with air expanding, as the workout grew more intense.

I was ecstatic at what I was witnessing. But I damn sho was not complaining. I could feel my own body begin to respond to what I was watching from across the street. I was in disbelief. My nipples were hard, my pussy was wet, and my hormones were running like a cross-country marathon sprinter. The next thing I knew, I was standing at the window touching and caressing myself as I watched that fine-ass man work that body, and damn was he doing a helluva job at it too! I was lonely because my husband was out of town attending a conference. So hell, what's a girl to do? I got so heated watching this guy I found myself rubbing and squeezing more and more as my body was responding to observing an early morning male spectacular just across the street. I could not believe I was standing there at the window half-naked with the curtains pulled back so far that he was able to get a glimpse of my actions. When I opened my eyes, he was watching me and smiling at the same time. I am not too sure how long he was watching or what he had seen for that matter because I damn sho got carried away.

After he observed my actions from across the street, he began to turn up the antics and put on a performance like you would not believe. I'm telling you it was like watching a hot sex scene from the hottest, most intense porn you have ever seen. I was embarrassed after realizing he saw what I was doing. I guess now, he feels like he had an audience, and that he must perform and put on a show as if there is no tomorrow. He put it all the way down! I believe he felt like he had control of the situation and that he must seize the moment to make me respond to him without hesitation. It was like, this is a damn drug, and I'm hooked! He would now take this opportunity to make my panties wet. While bending over during his exercise routine, he conscientiously spread his powerful legs eagle. He arched his ass firmly and bolstered his upper torso. I had gotten so damn hot I had to fan like a hippy in the Sahara Desert. The same thought played over, and over in my mind, Who in the fuck is this stallion? I mean, damn, I'm fucking standing at the window fucking myself while watching this man fuck me up completely.

I quickly picked up a magazine and began to fan slightly as I stood gazing at him. Of course decided he would add a few seductive moves since he had a private audience. He slowly placed the garment bag upon the brick column that was in close proximity porch. He also placed the suitcase nearby.

Now you can only imagine, with his hands free to move about, this fine ass nigga had the nerve to extend his legs as far apart as possible, with his hands extended vertically beyond his head. He stretched slowly and seductively. He slowly turns his perfectly sculptured body from side to side. He chose to bend forward with his perfectly shaped ass poised for the eyes of his private onlooker. You think my big pussy was wet initially. By now, it is dripping like a faucet. Still fanning and dripping pussy juice, I was not about to terminate this early morning unexpected spectacular view. After all, I had not experienced this kind of mental stimulation in years. He continued to seductively shift his masculine body in such a way that would only intensify my urge to have this man wrap those strong arms around me and hopefully feel that dick inside of me. I couldn't help but try to imagine what it would be like to experience a heated sexual encounter with this big black stallion who just happened to show up out of nowhere. By now, my tits were hard, my crotch was wet, and my mind was racing erratically. I was yet fanning trying and trying hard to control the urge of visual and mental seduction.

I just know that through his peripheral vision, he could see he still had a private audience. After a while, he had taken his suitcase inside, along with his clothes bag. Shortly afterwards, he returned outside with his briefcase and a couple of other items. He took this moment to stretch his body in ways any woman would absolutely be overwhelmed with thoughts of sexual excitement. I cannot stress how mesmerized and glued to my position at the window I was; not even a construction crane could move me in the wake of an emergency. I had locked every instance of his erotic behavior in my mind after noticing this hunk of a man flexing his powerful arms and working his muscles.

One of the most memorable movements he made was when he slowly placed his hands on his waist and began to move slowly in a circular motion that absolutely set my hormones on fire. I can tell you unequivocally, my pussy was on fire! I actually thought about calling the fire department to extinguish this blaze. I actually stood there at the window and watched him as he was getting ready to proceed with a routine of squats that are perfect for tightening the ass muscles. Each time he would squat, his ass would stick out in a perfect sculpted bubble. It was no accident he had his ass turned so that it was perfectly situated directly in my face. It was a shot of coveted perfection! I thought to myself, this black king has fucked my completely up! Call the law! I mean call the damn law now! Whew!

I thought many things at this point. I thought about how inappropriate for me to be at the window the first place knowing I have a wonderful hardworking husband. I thought about could this be considered a moment of desperation! I even considered this to be a damn joke for an intelligent woman such as myself being caught up in this type of behavior. I had to laugh at times! However, that would soon fade away after he continued to tease me with his erotic sexy body motions. After a few routine squats, he decided to turn toward me with his long legs opened and inviting my eyes into the center of his crouch each time he would bend to squat.

Only this time, his massive man tools were boldly facing me as to say, "Here it is! Come and get it." As he gazed his eyes toward the window where he knew he had a personal onlooker who was seemingly in a trance. He could tell I was melting in mental stimulation that was causing my mental faculties to become unglued. It was definitely clear this man was no amateur at dealing with women. He was well aware of his ability to impress women with his looks, body, charm, and sagacity. He was well-aware that he could be sexy and shrewd at the same time. I am pretty damn sure he would often play the women like a fiddle to get his way. He was indeed, a smooth operator. It was obvious when it comes to slanging dick, Mr. Man has the master plan.

He could sense that I would have loved to get a view of the actual male gift that he possessed between his legs. My eyes would not blink during the time I observed him lowering his body in the squat position. I managed to place my face firmly against the window in exhaustion from the intense morning unexpected workout I had just experienced. I think it would be safe to assert that I was thinking that this man had everything a woman would desire in a man. By now, he stood straight up and inhaled the fresh morning air. He began to breathe slowly as he relaxed after his morning workout. I can truly say for the first time in a few years, it is good to be home.

While standing, he grabbed his big massive dick and began to slowly stroke it in a slow vertical sexual motion. He turned slightly toward my home to get a quick peek at me, but I acted as though I was not interested in watching him. I was essentially trying to maintain whatever dignity I had, sense I was definitely struck with this big beau of a man. He was a very confident man. To say that I enjoyed watching his every move was clearly an understatement! He would just turn and wink at me and extended a smile. After all, Styles is a soldier in the US Military; he was trained to use his all senses in order to be aware of his surroundings. With time passing, he reached down and grabbed his briefcase and other items and went inside.

It wasn't ten minutes when he resurfaced wearing a pair of black athletic super tight spandex shorts with a black tight-fitting wife beater tee shirt. You could imagine I was now in a hormonal rage. He continued to maximize his workout routine by commencing a vigorous brief workout until his body was dripping with beads of sweat. His long black dreads were held in place with a black headband designed to catch sweat. You could see that the once clean, dry wife beater tee-shirt was now drenched in sweat. The obvious sight was the bulge between his legs, which was by all account a behemoth moving freely because he wasn't wearing any drawers.

Damn! This man has to know that his body is simply an amazing sculptured art form. Damn! Was he made, created, ordered, or what? I have never witnessed a man so perfectly built. He is absolutely incredible! Any woman would lose their mind for a man like this! It's clear that he has more than just a body. Just through an initial observation, I could tell that he is a successful and responsible man. Damn! I'm thinking about this man and reasoning in my mind as though I'm not even married. But I have to be honest with myself; it is what it is! I see what I see, and it don't hurt to see. In fact, a little looking here and there ain't never hurt nobody! I mean, a woman can fanaticize over another man without having to fuck him. If we are honest, we do it all the time. We just don't say anything about it. I mean, who can read our minds? Who knows our thoughts? Who can feel our energy and desires?

I've stood at my window and witnessed a sexual revolution in my mind from what I'm used to. I'm just thinking about it all. A gorgeous black man, with an incredible body, sagacious with charisma, and has the front tools to satisfy any woman. Wow! I mean, it's like is this creature of a man even real? I just can't believe one man can have it all! This guy, my god, I just can't explain how well put together he is. I mean everything about him is short of a miracle. His facial features, teeth, smile, thighs, not to mention his perfectly shaped bubble ass. Are all incredibly molded and shaped into perfection that goes beyond the ability to explain the reasoning as to why someone could possess every desirable feature. Even Hollywood would have difficulties explaining this. I mean, I have had sex with this man already. He is stimulating to me. All I can say is damn, damn, damn! I want some of that, and before it's over, I'm going to get some. I am going to taste every inch of that dick and ride the rest of it like Turner rode Trimble. That stallion is mine, and trust me, I'm going to ride that bitch! Call the law! Call the damn law!

Oh wait! The paper man just threw my morning paper! This is my opportunity to have a perfect reason to go outside this early in the morning. Still wearing my teal green negligee, I hurried to the bathroom and quickly finger styled my hair, brushed my teeth and sprayed a lil perfume on. I hurried to the door hoping I hadn't taken too long or too much time. I would not have been able to deal with myself if I had let this man go inside without me seeing him. Well, well, I was lucky, the black human god was still flexing outside. Whew! I mean, damn, there he is! Shit! He looks better now than he did when I stared at him for what seems like eternity. I mean, yeah, I saw him from a distance, but lawd, lawd! This man will set your soul on! All I can say is, "Somebody needs to help me!" Whew! I know I'm about to lose my damn mind.

"Good morning! Good morning, sir!"

"Oh, my bad. I didn't hear you, baby. I had these earbuds in my ears listening to my man Simone De. But yeah, hi, hello, wow! I didn't see you cross the street. But I sure am glad you came over! Thank you very kindly!"

"Your name?"

"My name is Styles. I'm returning home from Iraq. In fact, I just arrived earlier this morning and decided to get a lil workout routine in, just trying to stay in shape. My brother Meleak owns this house and I staying with him for a while. He's out of town for a couple of weeks."

"Ok then, Mr. Styles, It's my pleasure to meet you! I hadn't noticed you before coming out to retrieve my morning paper." All the time, I knew I was kinda splitting the truth. I damn near stood at the window affixed at what had captivated my total being. I mean, damn, I was breathless, totally mesmerized at this nigga, so much so until I had to think of something quickly in order to come outside and meet this man. It was totally out of my character, but hey, I had to do it!

"I didn't get your name."

"Oh, it's Nicole. I'm sorry, I should have mentioned my name sooner, but I guess I got carried away! I live across the street with the huge bay window. I love my picture window! It provides so much access for me to see wonderful sight very early in the morning. I absolutely mean remarkable and interesting sights. I certainly hope you don't mind if a lady gives you a compliment, Styles."

"Oh no! No, not at all!"

"You remind me of my professor at Alabama State University, Professor Moore. He was a tall, handsome, well-dressed black brother with tons of sex appeal."

"Seriously! Wow, you are comparing me to your tall handsome, well-dressed black professor with tons of sex appeal."

"Certainly, I don't mean to be too forward, or pushy you know. I did ask if you mind a compliment."

"Ha ha ha, no problem, no problem at all. I gladly accept your kind compliments, Ms. Nicole. By all means, you are a very beautiful woman, to say the least. So yeah, go ahead and compliment me as much as you like. I'll just eat it up! Huh! Hahaha, Nicole. Well baby, Nicole, I must say again that you are a gorgeous beautiful black woman. Now, I hope you don't mind Mr. Styles giving you a compliment. Yes, sweetheart, you are absolutely breathtaking!"

"Oh, Styles, stop!"

"I mean really, Nicole, your smile is as bright as the sun. Your voice is as romantic as the fire and light in your eyes. Wow! Nicole, this is a very special morning. So delightful to be greeted by a stunning goddess as yourself."

"Oh, Styles, don't be so dramatic. No Nicole, I'm telling you the truth. Okay Styles, I accept, and I must say you are right! Ha hahaha! I better be going, Styles. But I must say, you have really made my day, well, my morning."

"Okay then, I hope to see you again soon, Nicole."

"Goodbye, Styles!"

Whew! Let me gather myself! I must get a hold of myself quickly! I know this man was all that and so much more. This man is so incredible I almost lost my composure. I am almost ashamed to admit how seriously taken with this man I am! This is totally out or realm of reality for me. I mean after all, I am a married woman, a mother, a career woman, not to mention highly respected among my friends, neighbors and acquaintances. However, it took everything I had to keep from grabbing his perfectly shaped ass. I literally wanted to fall in his arms! I wanted to feel his body. I just wanted to take the tip of my fingers and trace his biceps and triceps. Damn, the man is incredible! All I thought about was having sex, even though a woman should be a little reserved, poised, and allow the man to pursue her. But nowadays, if you see what you want, you go at it!

I can't believe this! I actually cannot believe that everything that just happened! Wow, what an experience! This morning was like a fantasy, or a dream, I mean a sweet dream.

Must I forget that I am a married woman! I had literally escaped into a fantasy world with the black god across the street. For a moment, I had almost lost sight that I was married, not just married, but married to a very successful doctor. My love Kareem is away on a conference. He's due to return home in a week. I'm thinking to myself, should I, or should I not try and make a move on Mr. Styles? I mean, I have never felt so compelled to do something like this before. I mean, I know it's wrong, but it just feels so right. If I decide to pursue this hunk of a man, I must also consider the consequences of how things may turn out.

I'm back inside my home after getting my morning paper; however, I find myself back in the same picture window hoping to get another glimpse at this man. Damn, am I that desperate or what? Oh wait, he is back outside sitting on the porch. I have a million things to do in this house. I have errands to run, but I am caught up with this mental stimulation of having wild unrestrained sex with this man I don't really know. Shit, what's a girl to do? He's sitting there without a shirt on. I can see his big massive thighs gapped wide open, and that big monster dick piled in those spandex shorts saying, "Let me out!"

Got dammit! He caught me staring at him. He had the nerve to smile at me. I could see those pearly white teeth, those deep sexy dimples and that alpha male expression saying, I want to fuck you Nicole!

What do I do? I don't want to seem desperate or willing. What should I do? I got it! I will reverse the script. I will back my Mercedes out of the garage and put on a spectacle as he did for me. I entered my bedroom and opened my drawers searching for my favorite Daisy Dukes shorts. I wanted to really put on a show for him as he did me. I looked and looked, and finally I remembered I had placed them in the closet with my spring outfits. Very quickly, I got dressed and grabbed my keys and into the garage I went. I cranked the car, and as calm as I could, I pulled out of the garage and parked my squeaky clean sports convertible in the drive. Styles was still sitting in the same place. In a not so subtle hurry, I exited my car and walked to the trunk. I couldn't resist, of course you know I bent over, and over, and over, and stayed there for quite a while. I knew he was getting a full view of my goods.

I slowly picked up two items; one of them was pretty light, and the other could have had a lil weight on it. I walked around to the driver side of the car and placed them on the seat. It wasn't anything I needed, I was just playing the game. I wasn't use to trying to entice another man since I am a married woman, but hey, this really feels good to me. I took the same two items out of the driver seat and made my way back around to the trunk. I took great pleasure in bending over again and again in a very sexual seductive kind of way. I seductively moved my body to entice Mr. Styles who had a view that was fit for a king.

There was a towel in the corner of the trunk that Kareem would use when detailing my car on the weekends. I got the towel and slowly closed the trunk and began to wipe off the light dusty film. The car was basically already clean, but I needed a reason to see if I could get Mr. Styles to come over and offer a lady a hand. I pretended I had broken a fingernail, so during the course of me wiping the car, I let out a faint cry. Styles immediately jumped up and ran over to see what was wrong. I said to him, "It's nothing."

He said to me, "I heard you scream from across the street."

I said, "Oh, Styles, it's really nothing. I broke my fingernail! I believe it is cracked near my skin. It really hurt so bad."

Styles very kindly said, "Here, let me take a look at it."

He took my finger and began to gently rub it and slowly raised it to his mouth and kissed it. He said to me, "I hope you feel better."

I stood there and watched this man rub my finger so soft and gentle. I watched him as he slowly raised his hand to his perfectly shaped lips and very, very slowly touched his lips twice before lowering his hand and staring me directly in my eyes.

I said to him, "Styles, you didn't have to come over to check on me. I would have been alright."

"I know, baby, I'm sorry. I know, Nicole, I just had to come over and check on you! In my world, when a lady is in distress, you stop doing whatever it is you're doing and check on her, give her all the attention she'll ever need. So if I ever hear you scream out again for any reason, I want you to know, I will be there for you. Besides, the pleasure was all mine. I wanted a reason to come over to see you. Are you going to be okay, Nicole?"

"Oh, sure! I will be just fine I will be just fine."

"Styles . . ."

"Yes, Nicole?

"Thank you very much!"

I don't have to tell anyone that my pussy was steaming hot! It was wetter than a hundred-year rainfall in a tropical rainforest. My nipples were hard; my heart was racing. I mean, I had so much going on I absolutely didn't know what to do! I was totally caught up in the moment! Sheer passion had overtaken me! Before Styles left, he offered to finish wiping the dust off my car for me. As bad as I wanted to say yes, I just could not have imposed on him.

I said, "You are such a very kind gentleman, Styles, but I can't let you wipe the dust off my car!"

He said to me, "Nicole, don't be silly, baby, it's not a problem at all!"

I said, "Okay!"

He took the towel and began to fold it to create a distinctive fold so he could handle it more efficiently. He was very meticulous; I guess that's the military side of him.

As I stood there and watched him wipe with such intensity, I was amazed at the muscles that were flexing in his arms and all over. I was trying to take in the moment! His body was incredible, simply a machine at work. I have to be honest. I have never seen anything quite like it in my lifetime! Sweat was dripping and pouring off him. I immediately got up and grabbed a towel and began to tenderly wipe the sweat away. It looked like the more I wipe, the more ran down. He was hot, and I was too just seeing the sweat. I thought about a million things at that point; one of them was , well, how would it feel with that sweat running down the two of us. I looked him in the sexy beautiful eyes as I wiped the sweat. He said to me, "Nicole, baby, you're still wiping on me, and the sweat is gone!" We quickly looked at each other and broke out in laughter. Styles reached over very slowly and kissed me on the cheek. I froze! I didn't know what to do or what to say! I do know it felt so damn good. I stared at him and he slowly reached over again and repeated his action once more. I let it happen, I mean, I did nothing to stop him! I wanted it although I knew I was wrong, I just wanted it.

Just think about it for a moment. This big fine ass, handsome, black bulk of a goddess man whom I've been admiring all morning, has given me a feeling I haven't felt in years really. Here he is standing here in my yard wiping off my car shirtless, dressed in black skin-tight spandex shorts with sweat popping off him like damn I don't even know. Fuck! What's a woman to do? I didn't want to say it, but his dick is so huge I couldn't keep my eyes off it, and by the way, how can I when he's wearing spandex shorts? I mean, it's a woman's fantasy to have this happen to them, but this morning this is a reality for me!

Got damn, just when I thought I couldn't bare anymore, a mosquito bit me on the back of my neck! It was a painful feeling in a place I could hardly reach. Styles was still standing there of course. He heard me slap the back of my neck. In fact, he saw the mosquito, but he couldn't react quick enough.

Once again, Styles quickly walked to assist me. I ask him did he see a bump or a whelp on the back of my neck. He stood behind me and, with his massive hands, began to rub across my neck in a very soothing kind of way. His touch was soothing; it was peaceful and easing. I didn't really want him to stop. I could feel my heart rate increase. Once again, my body started to explode, I mean everything was going and doing its own thing.

When Styles pulled back my long beautiful hair and began to calmly kiss me on my neck, my pussy was once again wet and hot. I could no longer stand it. My clit was pulsating, my nipples were hard, and I was there for the taking. I could feel his massive monstrous dick pressing against my ass. Instead of inching forward, I began to press back against him as he stood there in complete control and dominance. Styles stood behind me like a towering giant!

I said to him, "It hurts! It really hurts, Styles!"

He then turned and looked at me with those beautiful piercing eyes and said, "I got you! I'm not going to let it hurt you too long, baby. Styles got you, Nicole. Just take a deep breath baby I got you."

After standing there for a while, we both realized the moment was spent and we both had things we needed to do. However, with a certainty, we felt sure we would see each other again, and real soon. For a Monday morning, it wasn't that bad after all. Somebody call the got damn law!

Now I'm thinking to myself, somehow, I got to move things along pretty rapidly because Kareem will be coming home soon. Styles doesn't know that I'm married. I don't know if he is married, engaged, dating or even cares about all that right now. I just know I got to get that dick, and I feel certain he wants me just as much! Wow! This shit is crazy! I got to get that dick, and more than likely, once I get it, I'm going to want more and more and more!

I must devise a plan. I got to come up with a strategy. I'm a woman, and this is completely out of character for me, but damn, it just feels so right. I'm not used to doing anything like this at all. But I have to make this work where he won't look at me in a negative way or anything. I am a very classy lady, but I got to have Mr. Styles, and usually, what I want, I get!

I have imagined Styles fucking me in every position imaginable! I want to have a rough role play scene with him where he has complete control over me. I think that comes from the fact that he is a masculine fit military solider. Damn, what's happening to me? I don't know what it is, but it damn sho feels so good.

With a million thoughts running through my head, I felt the need to share this with my BFF, Tamera. In one way I feel the need to keep this to myself, but on the other hand, something so powerful as this, honey, I got to let my girl in on this one! I'll give her a call at 4:00 p.m. She'll just be getting off from work. I must share this interesting day with her! We share and talk about any and everything. We have no secrets! She will be knocked off her feet! I know my girl.

The only thing I'm trying to juggle is Kareem is coming home soon. I keep telling myself, I have never been caught up in anything remotely like this before! I'm not even sure how Styles will feel after I tell him I'm married. This is totally out of the blue! Now I really know what our elderly meant when they would often time say you don't know what a day will bring! That statement rings very true for me now because I simply wasn't expecting any of this to happen. But it did, and now I'm here!

It's now 2:00 p.m., and I am trying hard to focus on the things I have to accomplish today. However, I am finding it very difficult to focus! I have to pay a few bills today and take care of a few other things as well. Right now, the only thing on my mind right now is Mr. Styles! I'm feeling a lil embarrassed. I feel like I lost control and never a good thing. I do feel terrible I must admit that. I do feel bad. I am a married woman, and Kareem and I have a good marriage, it's not by any means perfect; in fact no one marriage is. I have never had an affair on him or even entertained the thought. How foolish can an intelligent woman who has a master's degree in chemical engineering, a six-figure salary, and a husband who is a medical doctor, not to mention our two beautiful children, be? My home is stable, but right now, my mind is not! How could I let this happen? I guess deep down inside, I miss or long for the spontaneous attention Styles so effortless shadowed on me.

I see it's about 4:00 p.m. now. I'm going to give Tamera a call. She won't believe it! Damn! What is her number? She definitely will not believe what has happened! Shit! I can't even think of her number! I mean, I can't think of her number for the life of me! Am I tripping or what? I mean, I call her all the time! But here it is on this most interesting day for me in quite some time and I can't even remember the damn number. Oh, here it is, let me give her a call. I don't usually do this, well, make calls while I am driving, but this is the exception. I just can't wait!

"Hello, hi, Tamera!"

"Well, hello, Nicole! It's wonderful hearing from you, Cole!"

"Tam, girl, I had to give you a call to share so things with you that I have encountered in the past recent days."

"What's wrong, Cole?"

'Oh girl, it's nothing."

"I mean is something wrong with you or the kids?"

"No, we're fine!"

"Well, how about Kareem, is he okay?"

"Yes, Tam, we're all doing just fine! First of all, Tamera, I was a little rude when I called. I was so caught up in me until I didn't give you the opportunity to say how things are with you and your family. I am so sorry!"

"Oh, girl, Nicole, it's perfectly alright! I just what to be sure that you are doing well. It seemed urgent when you called and I just didn't know what to think."

"Girl, Tam, this is about girl talk!"

"Okay! Girl you know you can come on with it! Nicole you know I am all ears! What's going on?"

"Girl, it's like I don't know where to start! You know me Tam, you know how wifey, motherly, and conservative I am. Well girl, this man I met recently has absolutely blown my mind!"

"What? Not you, Cole."

"Girl sit down and tell me about it!"

"Wait a minute, Nicole, I'm getting a call from my employee at the boutique. She really tries to handle everything for me, but sometimes I have to make decisions only I can make. You know how that ownership thing works?"

"Yeah girl, I totally understand."

"But come on with it now. You're making me wait!"

"Well, girl, you know you and I have this thing where we oftentimes say you don't know what a day will bring! Well, honey, it's ringing true for me clearly at this moment in my life!"

"Nicole, girl, what is it! I can't believe you made that statement! What girl, tell me what's happening!"

"Well Tam, let me kinda compose myself, girl I am in another fucking world! I mean it! I mean I don't know what the fuck to do at this point! My damn mind is racing like the Budweiser Stallion!"

"Nicole, girl come on with it! You are making me mad girl!"

"Okay Tamera! Well you know Kareem is out of town attending a medical conference. Kareem Jr. is in college, and Jaylen is in the eighth grade, but they are on break right now. So really, I am enjoying this little vacation time. I wasn't able to go to Chicago with Kareem to the conference because I need to be here with Jaylen, plus I have a ton of things that I need to be doing at the house, so it was just a bad time for me."

"I totally understand Nicole. But you and I have been friends for a long, long time girl and I know it's something else going on in that head of yours; that's why we're best friends forever!"

"Tam, girl I'm trusting you with this! I must say that I am totally mystified at the fact my head is spinning with a million thoughts and I must say some of them may not be too ladylike, but right now this is how it is! Girl, Tam, early this morning, I was up, it was around 6:00 a.m., and I was walking in the living room to pull back the drapes. I decided to do it a little earlier, I guess I was feeling pretty good and I wanted to get a head start on things. Honey, I happened to glance across the street at my neighbor's house. I really don't know him too well but, anyway, it was a cab out front of his home. It had just arrived, so I decided to stand there to see who would be getting out of a cab at this hour. Girl Tam you would not believe what got out of that cab! It was the tallest, finest, most well-built, handsome man I have ever seen in my life! I want you to hear me out now. You know Kareem is all that and a bag of chips!"

"He hehehe, Girl you are crazy Cole!"

"No, I'm dead serious! I mean this tall black man was like a god or something! He was incredible to say the least!"

"Girl, Cole, are you serious?"

"Yes! I'm telling you know how serious this is. Girl, I stood there at my window watching him as he began to retrieve his items from the cab. He took his own time getting his things as though he knew he had a captured audience. I could see each of his muscles flex when he would grab an item, or just standing there holding it. After he got his things from inside of the cab, he walked around to the back and began to get his things from the trunk. Girl, when that tall ass stallion bent over to reach in the trunk, you could see his ass in a perfect shape bubble. He was finer than any man or woman! I watched him walk to the porch and put some of his things down, he had a long sexy stride that wouldn't wait!"

"Nicole! What! Girl, are you serious?"

"Yes Tam! I am damn serious! He walked back over to the cab to retrieve his last item out of the trunk. This black ass brother spread his legs and bent over, girl I almost lost it! I stood there as though I was totally mesmerized, in fact, I really was! Tamera let me tell you something, this man was so perfectly shaped! His ass was as perfect as anything I've seen! Girl, you know a woman loves a man with a nice ass on him! Ha hahaha! Tam, I am telling you the truth!"

"Nicole, girl, did he see you?"

"I am not a hundred percent sure, but I damn sure think he did. Just by the way he was flexing and shit, girl I really think he did see me. He kept taking his precious time and making all kinds of moves that were sexy and flirtatious, I mean they were damn right inviting!"

"Damn Cole, girl, what are you going to do with all that heat across the street from you? Girl do you think you are gonna be able to maintain?"

"Girl that's not all! About five minutes after the cab drove off, he came back on the outside and began to do some exercise routines right in perfect view of me. I'm like really! I know this damn man ain't finna flex his fine ass body right here in front of me while I watch, weather he knows it or not, I can't believe it! Well anyway, I'm like, I damn show hope so! I hope he is. He came out of the house with a tight ass spandex styles pants that were fitting him to a tee. Tam, This nigga was so damn fine I could never put it into words. I told you he has a perfectly shaped ass and his thighs were well defined, his arms were amazingly displayed in a tight-fitting wife-beater tee-shirt. Girl, Tam, let me tell you something! This man started to exercise in a sexy seductive manner that would have astound the greatest of them who claimed to have loyalty and discipline. Tamera, girl, he was built like a sex machine. I moved a little closer to the window and bam! I could see a pull in front of him that would have caused anyone to take a second or third look at what he had down there in his pants! Girl, this man had a dick on him that would no wait! He began doing some kind of leg stretch, and each time he would extend his legs I would literally want to melt on my own floor! I had a ring size seat to the be show I'd seen in years. When he stood straight up, and stretched his arms above his head, and spread his legs open. Girl I like to have fainted! This black king had my pussy soak and wet!"

"Nicole!"

"Yes, Tam, I'm telling you girl this has never happened before with me! Tamera, girl all I'm saying to you is, you would have had to be there to witness this god of a man!"

"Ha hahaha! Nicole, girl, what are you going to do? Damn! I mean I am sensing some kind of interest you may have for this man that I had never observed in you before, I mean not in the least! Girl, Cole, what are you going to do about this, it's looks to me like it going to drive to crazy until you can get some that dick! He hehehe!"

"Tam, honey, that's not all!"

"My goodness, is there more?"

"Yes, there is so much more!"

"Girl I'm all ears!"

"Well Tamera, girl this is what happened next."

"Cole, oh my sweet Cole, you didn't fuck this man already did you honey?"

"No! of course not, not yet anyway! He hehehe! To be quite honest, I haven't fucked him physically, but I have damn sho fucked him in my mind! I mean, mentally, I couldn't take it any longer. I have fucked this man ever since I laid eyes on him. Tamera, you known me for a very long time. You know how faithful, and committed to am to Kareem, but this is well beyond anything that has ever happened to me before! I really love my husband, children and career, and I won't do anything to jeopardize that."

"I know girl, Cole as close as we are, I have never seen you like this before girl!"

"Tam check this out, he went inside for a few minutes and came back outside and stood on the porch and faced me. I know within my heart he knew I was watching him, well he knew someone was watching him. I guess he just felt like putting on a show. While standing on the porch, his big massive dick was pulled in those pants literally with nowhere to go! He began flexing now from an angle of view that was perfect for me to see him. He did all kinds of sexy squats, bends, stretches, everything that could cause a woman to wet the hell out of her panties. Tamera, I'm telling you honey,. my pussy couldn't take it no more! I had to figure out a clever way to have a good reason for a woman to go outside so early in the morning if you're not going to work. Girl, Tam, my damn mind was racing. It was like I had to figure something out quickly before he decided to go inside. So I thought about retrieving my newspaper, or to see if they had dropped it off. I hurried to the bedroom and, listen at this Tam, I looked for my Daisy Dukes hot momma shorts that I only wear to the beach with Kareem and the family. I found them in my closet and I very quickly got dressed, and hand styled my hair,. I open the door and went outside. I even went to the curve and opened the mailbox knowing damn well I had gotten the mail out yesterday, but hell, he didn't know it. We have a large decorative rock out by the mailbox, and accidentally I bump my toe. I hollered out and faster than lightening he ask me was everything okay. I said in a whimpered voice yes, I think so. I bumped my toe and it is painful. He quickly walked across the street and began to assist me. He first introduced himself and Styles. He said he was the brother to my neighbor. I was at real drama queen at that time. After being that close to him, and looking this man in the face, I had only underestimated the sheer black masculine beauty of this man. We immediately looked eyes with each other. I saw him look me up and down. I did the same to him. He said, 'Oh! I am so sorry you hurt your foot." He said, 'Let me see it.' He stated he used to be a medic in the United States Military. He insisted on checking out my feet. He rubbed it gently and softly! I was like in heaven. This man has no idea as to how he is making me feel fight now. After about five minutes, he asked if he should get my husband or boyfriend to come out and further assist me to the house. I stated, 'No, but thank you, my husband is away on business. He is out of town for about a week longer.' I said to Styles, 'Thank you so kindly for assisting me!' He said, it's all his pleasure. He further stated, 'I delight in helping a beautiful woman like yourself.' We smiled at each other, and I said thank you again for being so attentive. He said, 'The pleasure is all mine, I hope to see you again, oh wait, I didn't get your name.' 'It's Nicole, my name is Nicole. What a beautiful name for a very beautiful lady.'"

"Nicole, girl, you have got to be kidding."

"Tam, I kid you not! I went back in the house and finished doing somethings I had started inside. I would say about two hours later I came back outside and I wanted to clean my Mercedes a lil bit. I backed it out of the garage and retrieved the soap and towels, well everything I use when I am cleaning it. I filled the pail with water and soap and began washing the car. Soon as I was totally involved in the wash, look who comes strolling across the street, Mr. Styles. He said to me, 'You didn't say you were going to wash your car.' I turned and said to him, 'I didn't think I had to.' So we had our first laugh. He said, 'Here, let me finish washing the car for you.' I said, 'No, I have it.' Styles said, 'I insist.' I said, 'No, Styles I got it!' He then reached over to grab the water hose from me. I said, 'Styles I have it.' The two of us ended up tussling over the water hose and which lead to the two of us getting wet. Again, we laughed that off. His teeth were whiter than white. I was completely taken with this man. I continued to wash the car and he would rinse. I took my time and made all the sexy, seductive moves while washing the car in the same manner he did me when he was doing his exercise routine. I saw, I observed him clearly, he could not keep his eyes off me."

"Nicole, girl, this is exciting! This is better than that Zane shit! Girl, Cole, I have to be honest I am quite turned on by everything you've shared with me about Mr. Styles."

"After washing the car, I began wiping it down. It was really my time to put my show on girl."

"Cole, you didn't!"

"I did! Girl, Tam, let me tell you something. I began whipping down that Mercedes Benz like it was a crystal chandelier. Girl, I tell you no lie! I reached across the hood and each time I whipped hood, I think I twist my ass right in Styles' face. Girl you should have seen that stallion of a man standing there looking at me like a dog in heat. I gave his ass just what he had given me with his sexual, seductive exercise moves. Tam, when I bent over to wipe off my rims, that when he really lost his mind. I heard him breathing like he had wrestled two sumo wrestlers. Honey I thought to myself, it's Nicole's time! A girl can play your damn game and beat you at it too! After I took a few steps back to check out what I had done so far, I walked around to the back of the car and open the trunk and bent over in the trunk like he did me. Girl, Tam, I was playing for keeps! I was in my zone of being in control of my situations. Tamera, you know how I roll honey. You know Nicole is going to be on top of things if, at all possible."

"Cole, girl I understand! Girl, Cole, what was he doing at this point?"

"Girl, Tam, you remember I told you he had on some spandex kinda stretch pants, let me tell you this. I tried not to look at his bulge, but damn it was too big to ignore! The dick was humongous! He tried to hide it a couple of times, I think out of embarrassment. I believe he didn't want me to feel like he was being too aggressive of too forward. But honey, that big handsome brother didn't realize that I knew exactly what I was doing, and it was working. I decided to take it a little bit further. I bent over again in the trunk of the car as though I was reaching for something. Girl, Tam, you should have seen your girl put the show on. I squirmed, I rolled it, I dropped it, I spread my legs as wide as I possible could to tease his ass like he did me. I then thought to myself, I know what I'm going to do now. Let me put on my boy Simone De's 'Tonight Is The Night' slow jam. Girl I walked around to the driver side of my car and put in Simone's CD and honey, I then looked at him and I walked back to the rear of the car to once again act like I was very busy in the trunk of my car arranging things in an orderly fashion while all the time the music was playing nice and slow, just perfect for the moment."

"Cole, girl, what happened then?"

"Styles walked around to where I was standing at the rear of my car and said 'Cole, ah . . . I mean, ah, you know, ah, well, ah.' I said to him, 'What's wrong Styles?' He turned slowly and looked at me as if he wanted to stick his tongue down my throat."

"Nicole! Girl you are kidding me! Cole! Girl, what are you going to do? This shit is better, in fact, it's hotter that 'The Young and The Restless!'"

"I know Tam right."

"Girl, Nicole, you got this man going crazy over you! You have got to have a plan of action somewhere like you always do."

"I know Tam. It's just this time, I feel kinda of vulnerable and weak in my situation. I feel like I have kind of lost control! Girl, Tam you know I love my husband, and nothing will come between us two. I'm just feeling, some kind of way right now."

"Well Cole, I don't know if I can help you on this one girl. I support you in whatever you decide, but this is a doozy."

"Tam, I'm telling you this man is everything any woman, or man for that matter would or could ever want in a man. He is simply more than incredible, he is amazing! I mean, I like everything about him! Usually, there are some drawbacks when you meet someone. But not this time. His teeth are pearly white, his smile is amazingly sexy, this personality is definitely on point, he has beautiful Jamaican dreads, his body is masculine and sculptured like a Greek god, and you already know I told you about that dick girl. If he doesn't have thirteen inches, he doesn't have one. I can't get over how nice his ass is. All I can think of is, in the words of Florida Evans of 'Good Times' is 'Damn, damn, damn!'"

"He hehehe, Cole you are crazy girl!"

"Tam, I was about finished with my car, but honey, you can imagine at this point my pussy was steamy hot, just by watching Styles. My nipples were hard, and my whole body was totally aroused just thinking about having sex with this man. I'm actually thinking about laying down with this man, and I'm a married woman. I have no excuses for myself. I'm just being real."

"Nicole chill, where do you go from here? I mean, even I would hate but love to be in your shoes right about now. He hehehe. This is so erotic, and so mentally stimulating, in fact, I don't believe you could find this kind of shit in a book. This is real like shiggidy here baby."

"Tam, girl I know! I have pondered over this and thought about it a million times. But for some reason or another, I'm still at the same place with it. Just as I was finished wiping off the trunk of my car, Styles walks over to the front at takes the water hose and sprinkle a little water on the hood, talking about he saw a few smears and he would like to make sure everything was perfect for me. So he took the cloth that I had and began wiping off the hood in a sexy, seductive, sensual, subtle, but very erotic manner. I actually believe this man wanted to give me a taste of my own medicine. He hehehe! I stood back watching him as he actually simulated a subtle lovemaking move while wiping off the car. The music was still playing. I had put in Simone De's new CD entitled 'Unbelievable' and it was now playing track ten which is a very sexy track entitled 'Talk to Me Baby.' That jam is hotter than hot! Simone De did that."

"Really Cole?"

"Yeah! He remixed it from his song entitled 'Woman You Are' and it's smoking hot! All the ladies love Simone De's music!"

"Really girl! I'm going to have to check him out."

"Oh yeah! Tam, you are missing out on some great classy soul/R&B style music like back in the day. Also, you need to check him out anyway because he is a hot ass, sexy artist. He's from the south, I believe Mobile, Alabama. But his music is the bomb! Anyway girl, Tam, Styles was working it so seductively and sensual, I walked up near him and he stopped for a moment and stared at me and slowly returned back to what he was doing. I really wanted to take a picture or video this man, but again, I didn't want to seem to forward or pushy. But mentally, honey, I have locked this stud in my mind for all time to do with him what I choose to. I mean. He's at my disposal, I am really falling for this guy. I observed him just about finishing up on the hood and on the sides of the car when a mosquito bit me on the back of my neck. Obviously, I was startled. I didn't expect a mosquito to bit me, but my quick reflexes caused me to kinda slap the back of my neck. Styles turned around and asked me what was I doing. I quickly told him a mosquito had bitten me on the back of my neck and I tried to kill it. He broke out is laughter. I said to him, 'Styles, what is so funny?' He said, 'Nothing baby,' in his deep baritone voice, 'nothing, I just thought about something.' I asked him why he laughed or what he found so funny. He said to me, 'Baby, I'm glad it was the mosquito that you were trying to kill and not me or anybody I know.' He broke out is laughter again. I said, 'So you trying to make jokes.' He said, 'Nawl, I just feel kinda lucky right now to now be on your bad side.'"

"Cole what did he do after your lil back and forth?"

"Well he walked over to me and said, 'Hey baby, let me take a look at it.' I said to him, 'No Styles I'm perfectly good.' He said, 'I know, but I still want to see it.' We slowly locked eyes and smiled at each other. Styles decided to give me a little personal attention, so he stood behind me slowly and very sensual began rubbing the back of my neck."

"What Cole?"

"Yeah girl! He did what! I'm telling you Tam, he walked up behind me and placed his hand on the back of my neck and began rubbing it, and girl, I can't begin to tell you how warm and good it felt."

"Cole, you have got be kidding me!"

"I'm not Tam! I mean I'm tell you the god truth!"

"Girl what did you do while this man was standing behind you?"

"You want me to tell you the truth?"

"Only the truth Cole!"

"I literally wanted to fall back in his arms. I mean, damn, it was magical! While standing there in front of Styles, I could feel his huge dick gently pressing against my ass. As he continued to rub my neck, I felt him getting closer and closer to me. He even went as far as to kiss my neck in a soft, sexy kind of way. I wanted to melt. I wanted to turn around and tell this man damn, please take me! I felt his warm lips again on my neck. My pussy was so hot I wanted to explode. His touch was so affectionate. Oh Tam, girl, I was in another world! My nipples were hard as hell. My knees were weak as though I was about to fall flat on my face. I literally could not contain myself. I began to breathe very slowly. I took several deep slow breaths. I had to maintain some level of posture. He continued to press that hard, massive cock against my ass. I slowly, but subtlety began to press back up against him. We immediately began a slow, gentle body dance without the acknowledgement of either. It was just kind of happening. Tam, I just felt myself take a deep breath to try to compose myself, but that didn't work. I tried to act as though Styles was having no effect on me. But clearly, that was working either. I kept trying to not loose myself emotionally. When all the time, I was going crazy over this man. I was giving in to him. My hormones were a wreck! Styles continued to stand behind me. His dick was hard and ready. I felt his massive, well defined arms embrace me with passionate, sexy caressing. I stood there in awe. I didn't move, nor did I want to. I was just thinking in my mind, I'm going to fuck this fine-ass stud. I was all in, there's no other way to look at it. I was in!"

"Girl!"

"Yes Tam! Styles stood there and said to me, 'Breathe slowly Nicole. Breathe slowly for me baby.' His voice was magical. It was like a smooth baritone, masculine sultry kind of voice, sexy would be an understatement. Girl, Tam, I mustered up the strength both mentally and physically to step away."

"Cole, honey, this is something! I mean, I'm fucking speechless!"

"Yeah Tam. What happened next? Chill? He hehehe!"

"Oh stop Tam!"

"Well girl you started it Cole. I mean, you can't leave me like this. He hehehe! Nicole, girl, honey, this isn't you at all. I am really having a difficult time trying to wrap all this around my mind. Cole, I have to confess something to you though."

"What's that?"

"This shit is sexy, arousing, and just a complete fucking turn on! Girl you can't get this shit nowhere! This shit is so fucking arousing Cole, until my pussy is hot as hell and wet like a motherfucker! Girl, I'm taking in all this shit. It is stimulating as hell. I'm sitting here just listening to you, and girl, whew! Nicole, girl, I have listened to you very attentively. I have visualized every aspect of what you said. Girl, I haven't had sex in a minute myself. In fact, I am holding back telling you how your very interesting encounter has turn me the fuck on now. I mean girl, it has really lit my fire. Now Nicole, you know you are married, and you are the perfect mother. I just want to know one thing. Where is the motherfucker?"

"Girl! Tam! He hehehe!"

"I'm dead serious Cole! Where is he? What are you planning on doing about the Mr. Styles?"

"Stop Tam!"

"Stop Tam my ass! He hehehe! I can't remember when I last had sex like that. Oh yes I do. It was with Sisco."

"Sisco! Yeah girl!"

"You remember I told you I met this guy name Sisco. He a fine-ass black man with everything a woman wants as well. I will have to fill you in on Mr. Sisco after we finish our lil girl talk. Nicole, I still see that look in your eye girl!"

"Yes Tam. I guess it's going to be in there for the duration now. I'm just kind of sitting here reflecting on the phases and drama of life. I know now why the named all the soap opera's real-life names and titles like *The Young and the Restless*, *As the World Turns*, *Days of Our Lives*, *Another World* because they are so reflective of real-life situations. Girl Tam, I never thought I would be torn between doing what is wrong or doing what is right. I guess in the case of love, the writer so eloquently stated 'If loving you is wrong, I don't want to be right.' Tam girl, can you really believe I am thinking about really pursuing this with Mr. Styles? He is just a different kind of man. He brings out emotional feelings that have been formant for many years. I guess too long people have decided to go along to get along. But after a while, things began to change. Anyway honey, we are scheduled to see each other soon. We have to weigh things out because Kareem will be home in a week. So I guess, like they say in the Bible."

"What girl? He hehehe!"

"Oh stop Tam! I heard someone say, whatever you gonna do, do it in a hurry."

"I hear you Ms. Nicole! I hear you honey girl."

"Well Tamera, I had to get over her girl to tell you about what's was going on with your girl face to face. This has kinda taken your girl here for a loop. You really never know what life will throw at you, but it's up to each one to handle it the best way they see fit. Who would have even imagined anything like this would have happen to me? I guess, like the older folks say, the devil is busy."

"Cole honey, have you decided what you gonna do about this? I mean, I really don't know what to say in a situation like this girl. It's kinda like, you damn if you do, and damn if you don't. I just don't know Cole what to tell you on this one. But you do know you have my full support in whatever you decide to do. Whatever situation you go with girl, I there for you! Just keep me posted my girl."

"I got you Tam. I better be getting back to my side of town Tam. I will keep you up."

"Ok Cole, I'll walk you to your car."

"Oh, no need girl."

"Oh, it's nothing Cole! I will be glad to!"

"I'm going home so that I can wash some of this pollen off my car. He hehehe!"

"Oh stop Cole! You just think this bad boy is going to come running across the street again. He hehehe!"

"Yep, show you right! When Mr. Styles comes running, I will be there to greet him!"

"Oh stop Cole! Girl stop!"

"Okay Tam, girl I will see you later. I better be going."

"Love you sis!"

"I love you too Tam!"

Well, I kind of got that off of my chest. I really wanted to share it with my BFF, Tamera. She has always been like a sister to me. In fact, she's more of a sister to me than my own blood sister. I know a million things are running through her head right now! He hehehe! Actually, maybe two million.

I cannot believe everything that has happened to me and all that I am feeling right now. It's like I'm in a dream! Yes, just going through life right now dreaming! Damn, am I dreaming? I must be dreaming! I, must be dreaming. Wow, it has really been a day for me. I am drained.

I wonder what will tomorrow bring? What will tomorrow hold for this girl? Hummmn! Should I go shopping? Should I go out and by a new outfit? Hummmn! Should I get my hair done? Oh yes!, I will get my hair done! I'm going to fix my lil self up and look like somebody. I really had a wonderful day. I have no regrets. I'm just going to let things fall where they may and go with the flow. Though I must say, I'm happy, excited, and delighted. Things have really worked out for me. Damn, am I dreaming? Okay, come girl wake your ass up and snap back to reality! Go back to the place in life before you met this god of a black man, Mr. Styles.

I guess now I will turn on my boy Simooone De and listen to some of that old school flavor R&B/Soul. That's my boy! That brother can sing anything! Where is that new CD of his. I know it's in here! Oh yeah, it's already in the CD drive. I played it earlier today. I want to her that jam he sings "Let's Do It Again!" I could listen at his music all damn day! In fact, most times I do. There we go! I got it set just right! Now, while I drive through this nightmare of traffic, I will jam with my boy.

Shit! I didn't know this traffic was gonna be like this! Oh hell yeah! It's Friday! People are getting off from work. Some folks are planning their weekend thang, and others are just out and about! So it is what it is! I'm not in a mad rush noway. I'm just cruising with my boy Simooone De aka The Bad Boy Gentleman of Soul! I can see him taking over the music industry. Once the right people hear him and work with him, it's over. I'm just thinking to myself right now while I navigate this traffic trying to get home.

I'm feeling really good right about now. Your girl is strong and tenacious. There's nothing I can't handle when I put my mind to it. Well, after driving ten minutes, I'm back on my side of town; everything seems quiet and peaceful. Oh damn look! That yard man has been here grooming my yard. I totally forgot about him! Wow! He really did an outstanding job. I am supposed to meet with one of my society clubs tonight, but I'm not so sure that's going to happen.

Oh my yard guy really did a great job this time. Hummn, he really took his time and did a few extra things. That's awesome! I love a fresh well-cut lawn. I love just walking around and observing the details of the lawn-care craft. Everything is really manicured so meticulously. I am really impressed!

"Good evening lady, Ms. Nicole, sorry to startle you."

I turned around to a familiar, sexy, soothing baritone voice. It was Styles.

"I hope I'm not imposing."

"Oh no, you're not imposing at all Styles. Good evening to you Styles as well!"

"I was out in the yard earlier cutting some shrubbery back and trimming so hedges, and I saw your yard man mowing the lawn, and doing a lil edging."

"Oh yeah! That's Jeff, he's our yard guy. He keeps everything looking great around here for us."

"For us? Yes! For my husband and I. Jeff has been with us for about three years."

"Oh, okay! Actually, I thought you were the one who was keeping things so perfectly manicured."

"Oh no Styles! He hehehe! I'm not above it, but I will have things looking awful. This is not my forte. Oh come on, No really, I mean it! I could not begin to groom this lawn the way Jeff keeps it. Besides, I might break one of my nails. He hehehe! See there, there you go. Styles you keep looking at me when I say us. I did tell you I am married right?"

"Well, let's see, was that before I came over, after I came over, while washing the car, holding you close, or hummnn? Let's me try to see when that actually occurred."

"Stop it boy. I told you."

"Really, to be honest, I don't know if you did. I have been so caught up till I'm like in another zone or something."

"What do you mean by that sir? Also why do you have that smirk on your face, like it don't make any difference? Styles! Why are you smiling?"

"Oh baby, I just thought about something that's all. I was actually just thinking and reflecting for a moment, that's about it. Maybe you told me and I wasn't listening. I don't know. But thing I do know it that you are looking good right now. Also baby, it would have been hard for me to believe that a beautiful, sexy, smart woman such as yourself would not be hitched to someone. I would never believe that you would be a free agent of a classy, elegant woman and not be married. That man can't begin to know how lucky he is."

"Well yes sir, I am married, and I have two children. I have one in college and I have one in the eighth grade. Oh how wonderful Nicole. I know you are a great mother to your kids."

"I absolutely try to be. They are my life! Well then Mr. Styles, are you hitched, married or tied up with someone?"

"Well, actually I'm not. Oh come on, no, really I'm not. I was married, but things didn't work out for us. We have great respect for each other, but things just didn't work out according to plans. Well, sometimes things happen in life for a reason."

"Yeah, you're right! Are you dating someone Mr. Styles?"

"Ha hahaha!"

"Why are you laughing?"

"Nothing baby. I'm not dating anyone. Actually, I just got out of the military. My whole life has been centered around my career. I guess now, I could be looking for a lil action."

"Oh, okay! Do you have kids?"

"I do, I have two sons. They are eighteen and twenty. They are great kids."

"That's wonderful Styles! I bet they are! They say the apple don't fall far from the tree. Why you keep looking over there at my flower bed?"

"Well your yard man didn't bother to weed your flower bed. I would have."

"Yeah right!"

"No baby, I would have! I used to do this kind of work. I owned a landscaping business, but I sold it to my sons and they're doing well with it."

"Oh, so that's why you have an eagle's eye when you are looking at my yard. I see you like to pay attention to details."

"Nicole . . ."

"Yes sir?"

"Hummn, now I could get use to that."

"I'm listening Styles."

"I have a proposition for you."

"What's that Styles?"

"I will give you my word baby, if you give me the opportunity to groom your yard, I will make it look almost as beautiful as you. Plus, I will assure you, the Yard beautification award with be placed on your front lawn. You see baby, everything I put my hands on, come out smelling like a rose."

"He hehehe!"

"Why are you laughing at me? I'm serious Nicole. I want to do this for you!"

"Oh Styles, I can't put this on you, we just met recently, and besides, Jeff is dedicated friend of the family."

"Baby, I mean Nicole, I'm sure you could handle Jeff in a diplomatic manner, and when it comes to me, I want you to put it on me. Trust me Nicole, it's no problem at all. Come on Nicole, think about the convenience of having a yard man right across the street."

"Okay Styles, I'll give it a try. I guess I will see what your work looks like. Who knows, I may have to call Jeff back if the quality of service is not up to standards. Now, you must know, I will fire you sir!"

"Oh absolutely. You would have every right to fire me if the work is not done right. I am a professional in everything I do Nicole, and I do mean everything."

"I hear you Styles, What's your price?"

"Baby there is no price. I just want to be able to make you smile, look good and have all around you looking as sharp as you."

"Styles, you know I can't do that! I can't let you work here free."

"Well let's negotiate Nicole."

"Okay what's on your mind Styles?"

"How about, the first six cuts are on me as a courtesy for you giving me the job."

"No Styles, I can't! How about the first cut?"

"No baby, that's not enough."

"Okay Mr. Styles, how about the first two cuts?"

"Nawl baby, you're really not understanding what's at play here. You see, If I mow the lawn six times, that means I get a chance to see you and be near you at least six days a week."

"Oh Styles! Stop that! You got to be more serious."

"Baby I am. I mean, I really am. Do we have a deal Nicole?"

"Ah, yes Styles. We have a deal."

"Okay baby, everything is settled. Thank you Nicole."

"No, thank you Styles!"

"We will talk soon. It will probably take a week before you'll need it cut again."

"Oh really, yes Styles, well, let me think."

"I could come over and start prepping the lawn and flowerbeds and treating the plants and trimming the shrubbery, hummn, starting tomorrow."

"Oh you don't have to Styles!"

"But baby, I want to. Now you gave me the job, please step back a little and allow me to create a masterpiece for you. Plus, I'm excited about getting to know things better around here. I am damn excited! You see baby, many time, all a man need is an opportunity to prove himself."

"Hold on Styles, this is my husband Kareem."

"Hello baby! How is the conference?"

"Wonderful!"

"I'm glad you're getting a lot of things done! I'm very happy for you and your team. Have you presented your presentation yet Kareem?"

"Yes baby I have, and they were ecstatic over my presentation!"

"Wow!"

"Yes honey, they were aghast at the information I presented on AIDS awareness in the public schools across the nation."

"Kareem, baby, I am so proud of you."

"So how have you been Sweetheart?"

"Well, I'm in my usual routine. I'm taking care of things on the job and here at home. The kids are fine. So basically, I been keeping things moving. All good sweetheart."

"You know daddy loves his girl."

"I know daddy. You know mama loves her hubby hubby."

"Yeah baby. Daddy can't wait to get home to his sweet cakes. I love you Nicole."

"I love you more Kareem. He hehehe! Kareem, Mr., you are the love of my life. I am a very special woman just having you in my life."

"No baby. Daddy is a happy and complete man just knowing I have someone in my life that completes me and complements me. I love you Nicole for that. By the way, Daddy got a big surprise for you when I get back."

"What Kareem?"

"Hummn, don't act like you don't know what I'm talking about? I can't wait to see you baby! Since I can't see you at night. I pull this big dick out while I'm lying in my bed thinking about you and I beat this big dick three or four times a night. Last night baby, I ain't gone lie, I shot cum almost across the room when I was thinking about you. I was watching my favorite porn and I just let it rip. Ha hahaha! One night I think the people in the next room heard me. Ha hahaha!"

"Oh stop it Kareem!"

"Baby you know how sexual I am. You just be ready when I get home! Daddy is going to smoke that meat. I'm going to set that apple on fire. Okay Cole, I better be going. Oh wait, I will call you a lil later tonight. I think we may have to stay over for a week if this doctor doesn't make it in form China. But I will call you and let you know. Talk to you later baby, love you!"

"I love you too Kareem."

"Okay Nicole, I wasn't trying to eavesdrop. I just didn't want to walk away while you were on the phone."

"Oh no. It's perfectly alright. It was my husband Kareem obviously. He was checking in with me. He said they will probably have to stay over another week if the doctor from China doesn't comes in."

"Wow, another week, with your husband away. Hummnn, I know that's going to be very hard for you. I'm so sorry baby. Is there anything I can do?"

"Styles quit it! He hehehe! You are being a lil silly Styles."

"No baby I'm serious. I know after a while, a woman has needs and wants, and if husband is going to be way for another week that might be a lil hard on you. I better be going, I got to get my workout in. I picked up a few more workout items, a weight bench, bar bells and a few ropes. I going to get a very rigorous workout in."

"Oh really?"

"Yes really. You sound like you don't believe me Nicole."

"Well I saw you doing some stretches and a few other routines, but I haven't seen you hard at it."

"Oh trust me, I do get hard, at it."

"Whatever! Mr. Styles, perhaps one day I could come over and watch you work out."

"Yeah, absolutely, why not."

"We could even work out together."

"I really think that would be just awesome Nicole, just awesome. I am sure I could show you few things that would be quite interesting, and you could do the same for me."

"I would like that Styles."

"I would love it too Nicole. I better be going Nicole."

"I understand. We will talk later."

Damn, What in the hell am I going to do? I am a fucking married woman, a mother, an executive, and here I am contemplating fucking another man as though it is the right thing to do. What in the hell am I going to do? I mean I have never, ever even remotely thought about anything like this, and now I am feeling consumed. I should not be thinking this way! There should not be questions in my mind as to whether this is right or wrong. I love my husband with all of my heart. But this man has my mind in a tailspin. He is so smooth, and gentle, but at the same time, he has this strong, masculine build and personality that I just love and admire. I mean, I love everything about this man! In fact, I'm kind of frightened at the prospect of a romance seeding and developing. I got to see this man. I got to talk to this man. This man helped me, this man touched me, this man caressed me, and before too long this man is going to be fucking me! He hehehe! He just left my house, and already, I'm trying to think of some reason to knock on his door and say to him, "Let's get it on!"

What should I do? Should I go over or not? Should I leave well enough alone? Damn, it seems I'm at the crossroad. What shall I do? Nicole go home, I hear a voice say to me. I hear another voice saying Nicole, go on across the street and get that hunk. A voice keep saying seize the day and enjoy yourself. Go ahead and fuck him! Damn, damn, damn! Shit! Florida Evans again! It seems I continue to reflect aimlessly on the moral of what's right and what's wrong. However, I continue to march right on towards it Styles like a roaring freight train.

Oh, wait a minute, my phone is ringing. Oh it's Kareem!

"Hi baby!"

"Hello Nicole! I just wanted you to know that we will be here another week for sure. The lead physician from China did not show up, he had to reschedule due to an emergency. So we're going to be here for sure."

"Oh honey, I feel for you. I know you're ready to come home. Is it anything I can do to make your stay a more pleasant one?"

"Yes, I'm glad you ask. I want you to have that pussy ready for daddy when I get there. In fact, I will call you and let you know I'm in route, and how far I am from home, and I want you to have that pussy out, no clothes, no nothing when I enter the door. Anticipate some serious hardcore fucking. Daddy is going to put a good fucking on mama when I get home."

"Kareem, you are too much!"

"You got me baby?"

"I got you honey."

"Take care, I will see you later Cole."

"Love you Kareem!"

Damn, I really need to call Tam and fill her in on the latest. But shit, damn, that's gone have to wait! I got to get over to see Styles! I got to see him, I must see him, I need to see him, and I'm going to see him! I got to lay my eyes on this big fine-ass man. All I can think about is watching that fine ass he has, that big dick piled in the front of his pants, those strong muscular legs and thighs, those beautiful pearly white teeth, and sexy smile. Damn I got to see him now! Damn, my pussy is so damn hot it's palpitating like a man beating a ball in the air with a rick-rack paddle.

Let me compose myself first before a knock on the door. I damn sho can't let him know he is having this kind of effect on me. I must maintain control of my situation. Let me take a few deep breaths first. Okay. Here I go. I'm knocking now.

Knock, knock.

"Hello Nicole."

"Hi Kareem, oh damn, I mean, Styles."

"Ha hahaha! You must have a lot on your mind."

"Oh no, not really, it's just an honest mistake."

"I understand baby. Hey, you really don't have to stand outside like this, you are more than welcome to come on in."

"Oh no Styles, that wouldn't be right for me to barge in your home unannounced."

"Oh baby, it's nothing really. Here, come right on in Nicole."

"I can't Styles."

"I really don't mind at all. In fact, I insist you come in."

"Okay Styles, only for a minute."

"I'm sorry to answer the door without a shirt. I had no idea you were going to come over. I never would have greeted a woman as beautiful as you with nylon spandex pants, no shirt, and no drawers. I feel so naked really. I feel exposed. I hope you excuse me for this. I apologize."

"Styles, it's nothing! I am perfectly alright with the way you answered the door. In fact, I think you are kinda cute, just a little. Before you go getting the bighead. I really do think you are a little hot and sexy too. Did I disturb you Styles?"

"No baby, I was just doing a little something to pass time. Oh my god! Styles! You're watching porn! Oh my! Styles! He hehehe!"

"So you find it funny or something. Well a man got to do what a man got to do! At least you have a husband to help you release your tension. Unfortunately, I don't have anyone that could assist me in that area. So I have to make it with what I have."

"Damn from the looks of things you sure do have a lot! He hehehe!"

"What are you talking about Nicole?"

"Oh nothing."

"What are you referring to?"

"Well, I see you're busy over here watching porn."

"Oh, yeah! I like to watch porn here and there. Ha hahaha! It's just something to help pass time, that's about it. It's nothing serious, it's just a lil some, some."

"Styles, you don't have to do that."

"Well Ms. Nicole, I never said I had to do it. When I get that urge, I choose to do it basically. I don't have a steady girl, so instead of experiencing with many difference women. I just select to handle my own business sometimes. Is anything wrong with that? You know a brother gets lonely sometimes. Just have a seat Ms. Nicole! I'm about to knock out a few more reps of sit-ups, push-ups, and sit-ups."

"Oh, okay, if you don't mind. I would like to see you work out. I think that would be interesting."

"Why is that Ms. Lady?"

"Oh nothing, just shooting off at the mouth I guess?"

"I hear you. Well, make yourself comfortable. I won't be too long, just got to keep the body in shape. I'm sure you understand that."

"Of course I do Styles, can't you tell?"

"He hehehe! Oh, absolutely! I can tell. I always start with my push-ups, but now can I ask you to please assist me with my sit-ups?"

"Really? What do you want me to do?"

"I would love you to hold my feet while I complete my sit-up reps."

"I guess."

"Please baby, I could really use your help with this."

"I guess so Styles."

"Thank you Cole."

"Cole, you called me Cole."

"Yeah, is that a bad thing?"

"Well, no, it's not, I'm just not use to hearing it from you. But I will be honest, it has a nice ring to it coming from you Styles. Now let's get on with the reps."

"He hehehe! Yeah you're right Cole. Yeah baby, hold them right there. That's feels really nice. Your hand are so warm and gentle."

"Thank you Styles! Let's get started Styles. One, two, three, fifteen, thirty, fifty, one hundred. Wow! That's great Styles! You are sweating profusely."

"Yeah baby, I feel like I have a few more in me today. Will you please assist me once again?"

"Sure Styles, I will absolutely."

"I'm going to try something a lil different this time. This time I'm going to lay on my back with my legs spread a lil further apart."

"Okay Styles, let's do it."

"Yeah baby, hold my ankles right here for me. Oh damn, that really feels great. One, two, ten, twenty, fifty."

"Oh, Styles, look at you!"

"I am sorry baby. I'm sorry my dick is hard. I'm so sorry! I tried hard to not let that happen, but I just couldn't control it. It's throbbing too. Cole I apologize bae."

"No, it is fine! If I be honest with you right now, you would see that my body is about to explode. My pussy is so wet! My nipples are hard, and my hormones are raging! I'm sitting here holding your ankles with your legs spread apart, watching your fine massive thighs and seeing how your dick went from soft to semi hard to throbbing hard. It has turned me on like never before. I'm like damn! My heart is racing, my hormones are going crazy, my mind is wondering and thinking, I'm holding Styles' legs with that huge massive dick piled in the front of him and all I can do to resist is fruitless. I got to have you Styles! I want to feel your massive cock inside of me. Styles, please listen to me. I have never seen a man so fine and sexy as you. I am completely taken with you. You are god's gift to any woman. I am so turned on over you! I mean, so much so, till I am almost embarrassed to say."

"Oh bae! Don't be embarrassed. I feel the same way about you! You are quite an amazing woman! I love everything about you woman! Your eyes, your ears, your mouth, your beautiful personality, your sexy body, everything, everything Nicole. I mean everything!"

"Styles, you have the sexiest ass of any man! I thought many time about grabbing it."

"He hehehe! Here, come here to me. I'm going to lay on the floor, I could use a great massage. Let me get the baby oil so you can pour it on my body. Damn baby, Nicole your hands feel so good baby. Oh man! I love the way you are working my muscles Cole, you are amazing."

"Lay flat on your stomach Styles, I am going to really work them for you."

"Thank you baby! I got you next. Oh damn Cole, I love the way you are working my ass. It feels so good bae."

"Turn over Styles, lay flat on your back."

"Okay baby. Oh damn! Cole you are amazing baby! Your hand are like magic. Your touch is like nothing I have ever experienced before! Damn baby! You are working my chest, stomach and my thighs so wonderfully. Oh, damn your hands feel so good on my dick baby! Yeah work that motherfucker! That's right baby, hold it tight. Massage it good for me Cole. Ah, yes baby, don't stop! Please baby, don't stop! Hold it tight baby. Yeah, massage it good for me baby. I love how you squeeze it babe. Yeah, move it up and down slowly. It's good baby, you doing it just right."

"Styles, your dick is huge! I have never seen anything like it! Not only is it long as heel, but it's fat too. It's huge Styles! How big is it?"

"I think it's about thirteen and a half inches give or take."

"Damn!"

"Ah baby, it's not really all that."

"Huh! That what you think! It feels so good in my hand Styles."

"Thank you for taking good care of him for me."

"Whatever Styles."

"Yeah baby, I mean it. I really needed this from you."

"Me? Why me?"

"Well like, I said, I have been watching you Cole and you are one beautiful sexy woman."

"Oh, thank you Styles."

"Give me your thoughts right now Cole. Come on baby you can talk to me."

"Styles, in my mind, I can visualize you making sweet love to me. I can actually see you sliding that big dick inside of my hot wet pussy. I am on fire for you Styles. I want you inside of me so bad! I have thought about it many times baby. I have even fantasize over you making love to me right after one of your rigorous workouts."

"Well baby, that is funny, because I have thought about the same thing many, many times as well. Nicole, baby I got to have you. You are whom I think about in the midnight hour. You are whom I think about when I awake in the morning. You are who I am thinking about when I'm going about my daily routine. I got to have you baby. I really want to love you here and now. Look at me Cole. I can see the fire and light in your eyes. I have not pursued because of your situation. But baby, I feel myself falling for you in a very special way. I can understand if you're not ready or if you don't feel the way I do. I can understand."

"Oh Styles, I have long for the tenderness of your touch. I have longed for you to hold me in a special way. I have longed to be close to you, just to see the fire and light in your eyes. I do feel the way you do. I mean I have never felt this way before. I can't ignore my feelings for you. Yes, I am married, but I am a very lonely woman Styles. Come here. We're sitting here on the floor having this conversation while holding each other close. I couldn't imagine any other place I'd rather be right now then here with you."

"Come here, hold on for a moment. Let me do something special for you. You put me on this."

"What is it Styles?"

"Listen, it is your boy Simone De singing 'Tonight Is the Night.'"

"Wow! Styles, you are so sweet. That's my boy."

"I think Nicole Simone is speaking to us right now. Listen to his soulful voice saying, 'Tonight Is the night girl.'"

"Styles, you're amazing. Thank you!"

"Now come here Cole. Lay down on your back. Let me take control of the moment bae. Kiss me Cole. Awe, so sweet. That's nice baby. This time, I want you to close your eyes and lose yourself in the moment baby. That kiss baby and your magic touch was awesome. Lay back baby."

"Ah, Styles . . ."

"Yeah baby."

"You feel so good on top of me."

"Just relax Cole. Here kiss me again."

"Oh, Styles, yes, don't stop. I love it when you are kissing my neck and ears. Oh, I can't baby, please, my god! Oh Styles . . ."

"Shhhhh, don't talk baby, let the moment take your mind. Cole, do you care if I get more comfortable and take off my clothes?"

"No not at all Styles."

"Well, only if you join me Cole."

"Okay, baby, I will join you Styles."

"Here, put your hand here on my dick baby."

"Styles, how big is it? I have never seen or felt anything like this, my god how big is it?"

"Ha hahaha! It's thirteen and a half inches. It's rock hard just waiting for you Nicole."

"Oh Styles baby, I can't wait any longer to have you inside of me."

"I cannot wait either Cole. Here hold on to me while I pick you up."

"Where are you taking me Styles? Baby, I'm taking you to my bed. I'm gonna love you good baby."

"Styles, I want you so bad!"

"I want you too Cole! Here lay down here on my bed. Kiss me baby. Hummn, yeah I love the way you taste Nicole."

"Oh Styles, you feel so good on top of me. Auh! Hmmmmn, yeah Styles, suck my nipples baby. Oh! I love what you do to me! Styles, your dick is so hard baby."

"Shhhhh, Auh! Auh!"

"Styles! Damn, it hurt!"

"Just relax baby. I'm gonna take my time. Just relax."

"It's too damn big, I can't! It's huge Styles."

"I know baby, I got you! I got you baby. Just relax and give me the pussy. I'm going to fuck you good tonight. Just let go Cole, let daddy take control. I got you baby."

"Oh Styles, my god! Oh my god! Damn! Styles! It hurts!"

"Take it baby, take this dick! You know you want it! You been watching me ever since I arrive. You've wanted this dick ever since you met me. I'm gonna fuck you good today baby. You may as well get ready for it. It's on."

"Styles wait!"

"Nawl, baby come on, ain't no wait! Open your legs wide for me. I'm gonna give you want you been wanting. Turn over on your side. Yeah, just like that!"

"Oh Styles, I can't take it like this!"

"Yes you can! Take the dick baby! You know you want it."

"Styles, you been fucking me for forty five minutes."

"Yeah baby, I'm just getting started! Turn over on your stomach."

"Styles, I can't!"

"Yes you can!"

"I can't!"

"Yes you can! Here let me help you Cole."

"Oh my god! Styles Ouch! Styles! I, I can't!"

"Let it go baby, let the pussy go! Give it to daddy. I got you! Come here baby."

"What Styles? I can't take it no more!"

"Yes you can. You are doing good. Come to the edge of the bed. Get on your knees and arch your back for me."

"I can't!"

"You can!"

"I can't!"

"Yes you can Cole. There you go. Good girl! Arch that back baby! Now I want you to relax!"

"Ouch! Styles! That hurt! I won't spank you that hard again. Auh! Auh! Auh!"

"Damn Styles! It really is too damn big for me! No baby, it's just right and it's all yours. Back up on it. There you go, good girl!"

"Ump, ump ump, my god Styles, you are killing me. I can't!"

"You can!"

"I can't!"

"You can baby. Just give me the pussy! You're doing good. Baby, my dick feels so good inside your hot wet pussy. Look here baby, I'm going to fuck this pussy! Now, we can do it the hard way or you can work with me and do what I tell you to do. Come here Cole."

"What do you want now Styles?"

"Get on your back and slide all the way down to the edge of the bed."

"No Styles!"

"Shit! Come here Cole! Damn girl! Don't play with me! I'm gonna beat this pussy up good for you. You want this dick? You want this dick? You want this dick, answer me?"

"Yesssss! Styles, I want it!"

"Kiss me, kiss me deep. Let yourself go. I got you baby! Come back down to the edge of the bed, do not run from me! Don't you run from this dick! Wherever you go, I'm gonna be right on you! If you try to run, I'm just gonna beat this pussy even harder! You can't get away. Just let me have the pussy. Auh! Auh! Auh! Auh! Auh!"

"My god! My god! Ouch! Styles! Styles! You're deep inside of me! I can't breathe Styles, I can't move! My god! Somebody help me! Auh! It's too big!"

Screams! Screams! Screams!

"Come here let me sit here on the bed. You get up on this dick and ride it!"

"I can't Styles!"

"We're almost done. Ride my dick baby."

"Oh please Styles."

"There you go. Ride it baby! Ride that dick like a pro! I got you! Ride it! That's right, grind on it! Harder! Grind on it harder! Go faster baby. Faster! Faster! Faster! Harder!"

"Auh! Auh! Auh! Styles! I'm about to cum! I can't take it no more! I'm about to cum!"

Screams more and more!

"Styles please!"

"Kiss me while you ride that dick! Get on your knees Cole and suck my dick. That's right suck it baby. Make love to it! Treat it like you love it. It's yours Nicole, you got to take good care of him now. It's all yours baby! Suck that dick. Put it all in your mouth. Choke on it baby. Suck it good for daddy. I got you baby girl. Look at me while you suck my dick. There you go! Lick them balls. That's right! You're a good girl. I got you baby! Come here lay back on your back again."

"No! Please Styles I can't."

"Come on baby, do it for me. I'm almost finished. Auh! Auh! Auh! Auh! Fuck! Damn!"

"Styles! You are killing me baby! I can't take it no more! It's too damn big! Please Styles! Auh! Auh! Oh my god! My god! Fuck! Right there Styles! Right there Styles! I can't! Please don't stop! You hitting my spot! My god, it feels so good! Please Styles, your dick is so damn good! Thank you Styles! Thank you! fuck me please! Please fuck me Styles! Please fuck me Styles!"

Screams! Screams!

"Oh! Cole! I'm cumming baby! Damn! Auh! Auh! Auuuuuh! Shit! Fuck! Whew! Damn ,I am tired!"

"Yeah Styles, I'm worn the fuck out! I can't even catch my fucking breath. I'm, I'm, tired styles, and sleepy."

The two of us lie here sleeping worn completely out, wringing wet with sweat! Breathing rapidly and steady like a marathon runner. Damn, Nicole is asleep after two hours of hardcore fucking has gotten the best of us! Shit! I am awake, and my anaconda is rock hard again. I am about to beat this pussy up some more. I enjoyed playing in that tight pussy. Well, it was tight, but it damn show is not tight no more!

"Hey Cole baby, wake up sweetheart. I know you put in a lil more than expected, but you did a great job baby. I want some more."

"Styles . . ."

"Yes baby. I forgot to tell you Cole, I have an extremely high sex drive. When my dick get hard, I want to fuck. You ain't seen nothing yet baby."

"What do you mean Styles?"

"Well baby, daddy likes to go at it. I like to work every muscle you talked about in my body."

"Baby, I wish I could Styles. I mean, my pussy is red and sore. My entire body still feels like you're inside of me pounding with overwhelming force."

"I got something this time that will help you to relax a lil better."

"What is it Styles?"

"Well, I'll let you know when we get together in the morning at 8:00 a.m."

"Styles, I had better be going honey, I have some things that I have to take care of."

"Yeah, well, me too. I need to take care of a few things myself. However, I will see you in the morning, right?"

"Yes, Styles, you will see me in the morning."

"Okay cool! We'll talk in the morning. Give me a kiss Cole before you go."

"Sure Styles! Oh by the way Styles, Kareem is scheduled to come home in a few days. I think by Friday."

"Oh, okay, that give us how many days to spend a lil time together, at least four. We had better take advantage of the time we have huh? We will make it work baby, I promise."

"Yeah, well, Kareem will be returning home is just a few days from his medical conference. I cannot wait to see him. I really miss him a lot. I really do love my husband."

"I understand Nicole, you should love your husband baby. I really understand Nicole. Your husband no doubt is a kind, special man. I believe you love him with a deep undying love. Trust me baby, I really do understand. I would never cast any doubt on whether or not you love Kareem, and because you are a priceless, rare diamond among so many others, I believe he has a special love for you as well. It is just a fact baby, that sometimes in life things happens beyond our control. Sometimes things happen and we are unable to give reason or explain how or why it happened the way it did. Look baby, I know you are feeling guilty right now, but the truth of the matter is. There is a powerful force that drew us and pulled us right in to each other. I want you to know that I would never do anything to disrespect you. Once again, I understand you are married. Let us just face it. Kareem is a damn much luckier man than I am because she gets to share holistically. I am not mad at my brother, he is definitely a blessed man. However, young lady, I want you to know something here and now. You are a beautiful, intelligent, sexy lady, and I wish like hell you would allow me to really get to know you more personally, and perhaps we could enjoy more special moments like the one we shared earlier. Look at me Cole. Look me in my eyes and tell me you're going to give Styles an opportunity to get to know you much better."

"Read my lips my black brother Mr. Styles. I Nicole have every intentions on getting to know you, much, much better."

"Thank you my sweetheart. I am going to fulfill your every desire. I am the man for you. We will keep it on the down low forever baby. I do not want anything to come between the two of us. Come to daddy. Kiss me Cole. Hmmmn, yeah baby, you taste so damn good Cole."

"Styles you taste and feel so good I love the way you touch me Styles. I love the way you hold me with your hands caressing my body so gentle. Styles, what is that? Auh! Oh Styles, your kissing me on my neck and in my ears. Those are my weak spots. I get totally weak in the knees when you stick your tongue in my ears and kiss on my neck. I just lose control baby. That' just what I want you to do. Oh Styles, hmmmn! Oh my god! Oh baby you are sucking my nipples Styles. You are kissing my neck Styles. Please, please, please, Styles you have your tongue all the way in my ears. I can't oh, oh!"

"Damn Cole. You pussy is wet baby. Let daddy finger that pussy real good for you."

"Styles, I have to go!"

"Come here let me pick you up."

"Where are you taking me Styles?"

"I'm taking you back to my bedroom."

"What are you going to do to me?"

"You already know what I got for you. I forget to tell you the code name for my dick is Thirteen and a Half. That's his name. Look at him; he's ready to get down to business."

"Styles, baby, my pussy is sore."

"I will take my time baby. Here lay down right here baby. Lay here in daddy's bed."

"Auh, hmmmn, Styles your ass feels so damn good."

"You like the way my ass is shaped? You like Thirteen and a Half don't you?"

"Yeah! I like it!"

"Lay right here. Open your legs I'm about to fuck you good again Cole. Auh! Auh! Auh!"

"Styles! It's too big! I got you baby! I got you! Tell me you like the way I'm long dicking you."

"I like it!"

"Say it louder."

"I like it! Let me pull it out so that pussy can feel the head of it before I shovel it back in there. Take that dick! Stop running!"

"Styles!"

"Stop running, come back here. Where are you going?"

"I can't! I can't! It's too big Styles."

"I'm gonna lay on my back and let you do the work. Get up on this dick. You can do it. Come on, get up there. There you go spread them legs wide open. Look at me. Look at me baby. I want you to grind down on this dick as fast as you can. I am going to make that pussy cream!"

Scream! Scream! Scream!

"Damn Styles, It is so damn good! Fuck me! Fuck me! Fuck me Styles! I need it. Please fuck me daddy! Ouch! Styles, you are spanking me!"

"Yeah, you been a bad girl. Now I have to spank that ass! Lay on your back bae, that's right! Let me get down in that wet pussy. You got some good ass pussy baby! Let me throw them legs over your shoulders. I'm about to fuck you now Cole. Yeah! That's the way I like it. Spread them legs all the way open. I got your legs over your shoulders now babe. Auh! My god! Auh! Auh! Give me that pussy! Relax Cole, let the pussy go!"

"Styles, you're all the way inside of me! Your dick is in my stomach!" Scream! Scream! Scream! Scream!

"Right there Styles, that's my spot! Please don't stop, don't stop! Don't stop!"

"Damn baby, come here, suck this big dick! Suck it! Suck it! Go all the way down on it. Look at me when you are sucking my dick! Get on your knees baby."

"I cannot."

"Yes, you can! I'm about to cum! Get on your knees. Auh! Auh! Auh!"

"Styles, You are killing me! My pussy is open."

"I know it is open! It has a big thirteen-and-a-half-inch dick inside of it. I know it is open. Arch your back. Spread your legs wide baby. Arch that back. Put your head down."

"Styles oh my god, you're hitting my spot! Please don't stop! Fuck me Styles! I'm cummin Styles!"

Scream! Scream! Scream! Scream!

"Damn! Shit! I'm cummin bae, I'm cummin, I'm, cummin!, Auh! Auh! Auuuh! Auuuuuh! Fuck! Dammmn! Whew! Shit! Baby I enjoyed that Nicole."

"I . . . I . . . did too."

"What's wrong Cole?"

"I'm worn out! I'm breathless! Okay Styles, I must go. I got things I need to do."

"I know bae! Listen to me sweetheart. I know Kareem is coming back in town soon, but I got to have you. You are one sexy, beautiful woman. Your smile, your eyes, your sexy body just turns me the fuck on baby. Every time I think about you nothing but happy and pleasant, thought run across my mind. I can't tell you how many times I have sat up at night or during the day and laughed when I thought of how you tried to play that innocent role on me like you were so shy."

"Oh, stop it Styles, I am a very shy girl."

"Shit I can't tell. Ha hahaha!"

"Well maybe that is because you take complete control of the situation and have no problem letting me know who's in charge."

"Nawl baby, it is not like that all!"

"Sure it is. Styles do you know I have dated other people before I married Kareem. I have experience intercourse with each of them. However, you listen to me, sir, no one, I mean no one has ever fucked me the way you have! It is without a doubt, you are a damn sex machine in every sense of the word. Your dick is bigger than anything I have seen, written, or heard about! You have a natural born behemoth! By the way, you are right to name it, or him, Thirteen and a Half. I am sure if you measured that monster, it would confirm every inch of its name. Mr. Thirteen and a Half, wow! Styles, I am going to get a shower. I need to freshen up a bit. I have to run down to the bank and transact some business for Kareem."

"I understand Cole. Take your time baby, no rush at all. I know you have things you have to take care of. I am about to get a shower myself and get a workout routine in. I thought about running today, but I will wait to start my running routine a lil later."

Oh, my phone is ringing. It's my girlfriend Tamera!

"Hi Tam!"

"Hello Nicole! I'm just touching base with you girl. I have not heard from you in a few days. I am checking to see if everything is okay with you. I know you seem very excited the other day when we talked."

"Oh girl Tam! I have much to tell you honey, but I cannot get into it right now."

"That's fine Cole! I wanted to make sure you are okay."

"Styles, I have to get going. I will talk to you later."

"Okay baby."

"Girl! Cole! I see now I called at the wrong time."

"Oh, it's nothing Tam."

"Cole I know you, what happened girl?"

"Tam you would not believe me when I say Styles and I have been spending time together. We have really gotten to know each other much better. He is a perfect man. I just like spending time with him."

"Cole, I saw the fire in your eyes when you talked about him to me. I watched your entire demeanor change when you would mention his name."

"Girl, Tam, I cannot explain this feeling. I guess it's much like my boy Simone De when he sang 'Take my hand, come with me baby to love land, let me show you how sweet it could be, sharing your love with Simone De but it feels so good, when you're loving, when you're loving someone.' Simone De said that shit, and it's real!"

"Well Cole are you planning to fuck him?"

"Tam, girl you late! That fine, black, sexy, big dick motherfucker has literally fucked the hell out of me!"

"What?"

"Yes! Tam I am serious! Girl, I can hardly walk!"

"Nicole!"

"Tam, I'm trying to tell you girl. Styles is a damn sex machine that works dramatically in overdrive. Girl, Tam, He is ridiculous in bed. He is unbelievable to say the least. Girl, he put my body in positions I never thought would be possible. He fucked me one time for two hours straight!"

"What! Damn Cole!"

"Yes girl. That stallion can slang some dick! He's dominant in bed. He ask no questions, and he doesn't take no for an answer."

"Cole, my god girl! Did you say the first time?"

"Yes, the first time."

"How many times has he laid pipe to you girl?"

"Tam it was two times, but I have to get something from him a lil later today."

"Sure!"

"I do girl."

"And what is that?"

"Some more of that dick girl. That man had me on my knees sucking that big monster!"

"Cole, my girl is swallowing dick now!"

"He hehehe! Girl, I'm telling you, he leaves you no choice. Tam, girl you know I shared an experience with you once about Kareem. I told you how he would fuck me in every room in the house, and he can really work that dick, and mind you he is eleven inches himself and dangerous with it. Well girl, there is no one I can even begin to compare Styles to. He is in a class all by himself. He is a master at fucking! He has thirteen and a half inches Tam!"

"What! Goddamn girl, it is a wonder you are able to walk! When will Kareem be home Cole?"

"In less than a week he should be back home Tam."

"Did you tell Styles about Kareem? Yes, I did, he fully understands that I am married and I not going anywhere."

"Okay, as long as he understands."

"Girl we should go out tonight."

"I can't!"

"Why?"

"Well I have so much to do Tam, I have to do a lil work at home, you know tidy up a few things before Mr. Kareem gets home."

"What about later?"

"Well Tam, you know, I just have so much to do."

"Girl, Ms. Cole, you know why you can't go. You got to meet Mr. Styles tonight."

"Not really Tam."

"I think so girl, but I damn sho understand!"

"Hold on Tam, wait a minute, he's in the yard."

"Hi Styles!"

"Hey bae. I was wondering if you could come over a lil later and help me with something."

"I'm not sure Styles, I have so much to do! Please bae, It won't take too long. Can you please do that for me?"

"Okay Styles, you win!"

"Cool, thank you Cole. How about around 8:30?"

"Sure, okay, that would be fine!"

"Here is my number Cole. Call me, and let me know you're on your way."

"Okay Styles, I will."

I need to run to the mall and pick up a few items, then go by the grocery store to get a few things as well. I have a taste for a steak tonight. I will pick up a couple of porterhouse steaks and grill them.

Wow! My my. Time just flies, I mean, I spent all day in the store it seems. I'm tired, but I can't let Styles down. I am exhausted. I'll be fine once I get a hot shower. It's 7:30 p.m. already! I can't believe it! Time has flown by! Wow!

Let me give Styles a call and see if I can just see him tomorrow.

"Hello."

"Hi Styles. Are you asleep Styles?"

"Oh no bae. I was just sitting here waiting on you to call. Are you coming over to spend a lil time with me? I know you're tired bae."

"Yeah, I am, I picked up a couple of porterhouse steaks to grill at your place, but we can do that another time."

"Yeah bae, that was so thoughtful of you! Since it's kinda late, we can grill maybe tomorrow. I really want to see you! Hey when you come over, just come on in, I will probably be in the shower, so the door will be unlocked, just come on in."

Knock, knock.

"Styles, I'm coming in sir. Wow! Styles it smells so good in here! Oh look at the beautiful rose petals so perfectly displayed. Oh the music is beautiful. Styles, where are you? I know he's here somewhere. Styles! Where are you? I know you are here. Oh my, the petals are lovely! Now where do they lead? I'm just going to follow them. He's not in here. He's not in here! Let me check the bedroom. The light is dim, and I see a beautiful candle burning. Let me see if he is in here. Oh my god Styles. You're sitting there with no clothes on! Styles! You know how weak I am for you. You're sitting there naked with your dick hard as a brick, and your legs spread wide open. Oh baby, Styles, when I see you like that, it makes me want to have you!"

"Come here Nicole! Come here baby. Get down on your knees, look at me, and kiss me. Don't stop baby. Stick your tongue all the way down my throat."

"Oh Styles, my pussy is so wet! My nipples are so hard honey."

"Shhhh! Suck my dick. Suck it, that's right lick it! Look up at me while you are sucking my dick. Kiss the head. I want you to do what I tell you to do Cole. Take your clothes off."

"Styles, I can't stay!"

"Take your clothes off now."

"Okay Styles."

"Don't question me baby. Just do what I tell you to do. Take everything off. Damn baby, you are so damn fine! Dance for me, I want you to do an erotic sexual dance for me. Take your hand, touch your lips, touch your nipples. Good. Now touch your pussy. Play in that pussy. Play in it! Make that pussy wet! Come here, turn around. I want to see that ass. Back up ,all the way up. Close your eyes, come here. I will guide you baby. That's right! Sit on this dick."

"Oh Styles, I can't!"

"Yes you can. Sit on this dick Cole."

"Oh my god! It's too big!"

"Here, drink this. It will help you relax."

"Auh! My god Styles! Your dick is too big baby."

"Drink some more of this."

"What is it? It's nothing, just drink it. I got you. I got you baby. Drink some more."

"Oh Styles, I'm feeling so good! Oh Bae, I feel like I can fly! I'm really feeling damn good. Auh! Yeah, give me that dick Styles! It was hurting, but now it feels so damn good. Fuck me Styles! Please! Fuck me baby!"

"Ride the dick baby. Ride daddy's dick good for me. Can you ride it good for me?"

"Yes, yes daddy! I can ride it! Ride it then! Grind on that dick! You said you feel good now, grind it hard! Fuck me Nicole! Fuck me good baby!"

"My god, it so deep inside of me! I love your dick! I love your dick! I love your dick Styles! Please fuck me harder Styles!"

"Whose pussy is this Cole?"

"Yours."

"Whose pussy?"

"It's your pussy Styles!"

"Fuck me then! Give it to me baby! Let yourself go! Give me the pussy! Let daddy fuck you good!"

"Okay! I will! I will give you my pussy. I'm gonna cum! I'm gonna cum! I'm gonna cum!"

Scream! Scream! Scream!

"Damn! It's so good baby!"

"Come here Cole. We're just getting started! Suck that dick! What's my name?"

"Styles!"

"What's my name?"

"Styles! Styles!"

"Swallow that dick!"

"Styles! Styles! My god!"

"Suck my dick! Kiss the head! Make love to it. Look at that dick, worship it. Love it! Love it! Kareem may be coming home, but this pussy belongs to me. I'm gonna fuck you when I want to. You hear me?"

"Yes!"

"I can't hear you."

"Yes Styles! It's your pussy!"

"Now suck that dick good for me! Suck it like you love it. Move your hands, swallow that dick. Let me see your eyes! I'm gone fuck you like you never seen before. Lick my balls! Slowly lick them. Put both of them in your mouth! Now put that dick back in your mouth. Come here. Kiss me! Stick your tongue all the way down my throat. Let yourself go! I got you! I got you bae. Love it! Loooove it! Come here, lay on your back. Open your legs."

"Styles, I'm tired and sore from earlier."

"I know, but you need to be fucked! Do what I tell you baby. Open your legs. Auh! Auh! Auuuh!"

"Styles! It's so big! I can't!"

"Yes you can baby. You can do it. Just relax, and give it to me, Give me the pussy! Let yourself go. I got you!"

"Auh! Auh! Damn! Oh my god! It's so deep inside of me! I feel it in my guts!"

"You ain't seen nothing yet baby. Put your arms over your head, and leave them there!"

"Auh! My god!"

"Try this, it should relax you. Try it again, it should kick in in a minute."

"Hmmmn, I'm feeling so good Styles! Fuck me please."

"Yeah, I'm about to honor that. Kiss me Cole. You feel that dick in you? You feel all of it?"

"Yeah! It's deep inside of me Styles. Just open your legs baby. Let me in. Let me fuck you good tonight. Yeah Nicole, that's how I like it! Damn, baby, I'm in that pussy! It's open too! Shit! You like the way I long stroke that pussy?"

"Oh Styles, your dick is so good to me! Please don't stop! Please don't stop! Fuck me Styles, You got my legs bent over my head! Oh my god! I'm about to cum! I'm about to cum!"

Scream! Scream! Scream! Scream! Scream!

"Oh no, don't pass out now. I'm just getting started baby! Turnover on your stomach!"

"I can't Styles, I'm so tired."

"Here try a lil more of this it will help you. Lay on your stomach. Spread your legs wide as you can. When you can't spread them anymore, I'll do the rest. I'll spread them! Here put this pillow under you. That's right! That's how I like to see that ass in the air. Reach behind you and grab this dick. Stroke it! Keep stroking it! Wait a minute, let me get that oil. I want to put it all over your back so I can just slide around until I slide right back in that pussy. Auh! I just have the head in it bae. Kiss me. I know it makes that pussy wetter. Kiss me!"

"Oh Styles, you have your tongue in my ears, that drives me crazy Styles! It drives me crazy. I look all sense of control when you put your tongue in my ear and you kiss me on my neck!"

"I know that baby, that's why I have you in this position."

"Oh Styles, you have your tongue in my ear!"

"Give daddy that pussy! Give it to me! Give me all of it Niocle! There you go! I'm deep in that pussy now! I'm just gonna fuck you till I get tired."

"Hmmmn, hmmmn, hmmmn, oh my god. Yeah! It feels so good! I need you Styles! I need to feel your dick inside of me! Right there! Keep it right there, don't stop! Please don't stop Styles! I'm about to cum!"

"Go ahead, cum baby, go head on and cum while I beat this pussy down. Oh my god, I'm cummin! I'm cummin! I'm cummin! I can't stop!"

Scream! Scream! Scream!

"Let it go baby, just let it go. Get on your knees Cole."

"I can't Styles!"

"Yes you can. Get on your knees and arch that back! Spread those legs and arch that back! Head down, ass up! That's the way I like to fuck! Back up on this dick! Work it! Work it! Don't stop, keep going! Keep going! Didn't I tell you not to stop! Back that ass up! Now grind that dick, don't stop! Grind that dick good! Shit! This pussy is good! Damn baby, This pussy is good. Here you go bae."

"No Styles, I got to go! I have so much to do! I got to go now."

"I understand bae. Let me lay down so you can ride this dick before you go. Get on this big dick. I want you to fuck me good, or we gone start all over again. Come on Cole, I'm gonna lay like this until you make me cum. That's right ride it baby! Faster, faster, harder, harder! Grind it! Grind it harder! Come up to the head of that dick. Come all the way to the head of that dick! Open your eyes! Throw your head back while you are riding this dick! Wait a minute, I want you to squat, that's right squat come all the way down, then back up. Keep doing that. Shit! This pussy is good! Oh my fucking god! Oh my fucking god! Fuck me!"

"Styles! Your dick is huge, I don't think I can take it anymore!"

"You want me to stop?"

"No! Please don't stop! I love your dick! I love your dick!"

"Whose pussy this is?"

"It's your pussy!"

"Whose pussy this is?"

"It's your pussy Styles!"

"Well fuck me like it's my pussy! You want me to give this dick to someone else?"

"No! Please don't give your dick to someone else Styles! Please don't give your dick to someone else! I love your dick!"

"Well fuck me then! Here wait a minute, here try this again."

"Okay, I will! Oh my fucking god! I feel so good! Fuck me harder Styles!"

"Why you crying baby? Cole why you crying?"

"The dick is so good! I feel you all the way in my stomach! You are beating my guts in Styles! Auh! Auh! Auuuh! Auh! Auuh!"

Scream, scream, scream, scream!

"Damn! Damn! My god, I'm cumming! I'm cumming Styles! Styles! Oh my!"

Screams!

"You ready for this nut, here it comes auuuuuh, auuuh, damn, damn, auuuh, shit, shit! Damn baby! That pussy is the bomb! Whew! Damn, I'm out of breath! Are you okay Cole?"

"My god, I have never been fucked like that a day in my life! I have never heard of anyone being fucked like that a day in my life. I don't know of anyone being fucked like that a day in anyone's life!"

"Oh come on Cole."

"No! I am serious! My god Styles. I better get going if I can. I don't know if I can walk after all of that."

"Oh, you just talking. You just talk young lady. I will say, I really enjoyed you baby. I hope to see you again soon. Give me a kiss before you go. Auh, that was nice. I'll see you later, take care."

Damn, my phone has been ringing. I wonder who was calling. I was too caught up in the moment to answer the phone. Shit six missed calls. Oh, three of them were Kareem. Damn, I had better think of something fast! I had better call him to see what his plans are. I am going to get a shower first. No, I better give him a call before he start to act suspicious. Wait a minute! Hey, Kareem is already home! What a surprise! I damn sure was not expecting that, not tonight!

"Surprise baby!"

"Oh Kareem, you're home! Wow! I didn't expect you home so soon! I can't believe it!"

"Baby, you act as if I was not supposed to come home."

"Oh no honey, I am glad to see you! I am happy you are here! Welcome home honey! It is just I was not expecting to see you tonight. Here honey, let me help you, give me this bag. Sit down baby. Welcome come home Kareem!"

"Hey Cole, where were you? I noticed your car was in the garage and your keys and purse was still here."

"Oh, I was assisting our neighbor Janice with some paperwork."

Fuck! What do I do now? I was not expecting Kareem tonight and here he is talking about surprise! I am glad to see him, but damn! I just received the most aggressive, dominant fucking of a lifetime from a man whom I have only known for a short period, and my husband has just arrived home after being gone for almost two weeks. I hope he has taken advantage of beating that dick because I cannot take anything tonight. I mean not even a tongue. I was planning on taking a bath and soaking my pussy in some alum water to hopefully tighten it back up. I have been fucked for hours with a big black bulk of a man with the biggest dick I've ever seen. Not to mention Kareem is certainly not short changed in that area at all. He has a big dick that will not wait as well. He is not as dominant and rough as Styles, but he is definitely all man, knows how to use it, not only that, but the loves to use it. Damn, damn, damn, I knew Kareem would be coming home soon, maybe in a couple of days. However, I had absolutely no idea he could be here tonight. I was gonna put this pussy of ice and let it rest and recuperate some before Kareem got home. Damn, I just need a few moments to get myself together. I need to gather my thoughts and get back on track and a mother and wife. Fuck!

I am still in disbelief that I even engaged in this situation to start with. Styles has consumed my mind, every single thought. Now reality has set in, my husband is home, and I have to get back to being a wife again. I'm gonna jump in the shower and freshen up a bit and come out and spend some time with Kareem.

"Hello Dear!"

"Hi Kareem! I'm so glad you're home baby. It's been so lonely with you being away. The kids are away on retreats and I have been here just doing my normal routine. This house has not been the same since you been away."

"Oh Nicole, don't be so modest."

"No Kareem. I really mean it! I missed you Kareem!"

"I missed you too Cole! I love you baby."

"I love you too! Tell me about your conference Kareem."

"Well, first, those meetings are getting longer and longer. In fact, it seems like the walls are closing in while listening to some of the medical experts."

"Oh honey, I hate to hear you had to endure the agony of being bored while away from home."

"Well, not all of it was boring. Actually most of it was informative and exciting new breakthroughs. There were many twenty-first-century techniques discussed and implemented for patients' care and maintenance on various disease."

"Usually when you're away, I hear quite a bit from you. But I took it as though you were busy and would check in when you could. I don't like to crowd you while you're away attending a conference."

"I understand Cole. I really do appreciate your kind consideration. You are the perfect wife, that's why I love you so much."

"Oh Kareem, thank you!"

"Yeah baby, we had a full agenda this time. We had get-acquainted events, sometime I could hardly stay awake because the premedical conference with the doctors were grueling. We had to stay late for those. Each night I would go back to my hotel room to shower and check my messages from the office. You know how the dictating process works. I have to make sure all that stuff is prioritized and catalogued."

"Oh sweetie, Kareem I understand! I love you so much, and I am very happy to have you home."

"Thank you Cole. I really love you."

"I love you too baby."

"Tell me how have you been keep yourself. I want to hear all about it."

Shit, no you don't.

"My lil pudding, my precious heart, tell me about your week. Sit down and tell daddy what you been up to. Don't leave anything out. I'm all ears baby."

"Oh Kareem, my week was routine. I didn't do too much just my usual house duties and I complete a few projects from work. I got a chance to work out quite a bit at the gym trying to stay in shape."

"Yeah baby, you told me you were going to start your workout routine soon. That's great! I'm so proud of you. I can see right now that you have really been working out big time! Come here, let me check you out. Looks like I can see some positive results already!"

"Oh stop Kareem! You can't see anything yet. He hehehe! I just started sir. It's going to take a minute before you can see any results."

"Okay baby, I just wanted to be positive, you know how I am ha hahaha!"

"Thank you sir!"

"Well your body is perfect in every way. I'm about to get a shower Cole and kinda relax a little. I feel like being a bad boy tonight! In the words of your boy Simone De, 'You gonna make me a bad boy!'"

"Baby, I know you are probably too tired for that tonight Kareem. No baby, I been waiting and counting down the days! Just try and get some rest tonight baby, mama knows her daddy is tired."

Damn, I'm worn the fuck out! What the fuck! Maybe I can just keep him talking about his trip and he'll fall asleep.

"Yeah, I am tired Cole. You are so kind to me. You are the kind, sweet, sexy wife that I married, that is why I love you so much! You are the light of my life."

"Kareem you are too sweet."

"No baby, I been gone and I feel guilty for leaving you. I want you to know that I will make it up to you. That's why, when I shower, and get a bite to eat. I want some serious sex tonight, plus that thang ought to be good and tight for me. I know you miss this dick too Nicole. I understand you are concerned about my state of rest right now, but I wants to fuck tonight! I know you been missing Daddy too. I'm gonna make it up to you. I know your body all too well Cole. Whenever I'm away attending my conferences, I can easily tell your body's reaction towards me. I love how that pussy grips my dick after being away for a while. Now be a good girl for Daddy and go get that pussy ready for me."

"Okay Kareem."

Shit! Damn! I'm fucked! I'm not believing this shit, not all over again! I wonder if this man will be able to tell if my pussy is loose and shit. What a fucking coincidence; not only have I been fucking another man, but I been fucking another man with the biggest dick in the fucking country looks like. Styles has a fucking horse dick, and he has made damn sure that he gave me every inch he had more time over. My fucking insides are still sore, my lips are fucking ruptured and shit, they ought to be deflated by now. My nipples are sore as hell, and I am sure I am open like the Grand Canyon.

I am married to Kareem. I love this man dearly. I am preparing myself both mentally and physically to satisfy may husband, as I should. Kareem, who always engages in sensual foreplay by kissing me on the neck, rubbing his hands up and down my body, licking my ears and sucking on my nipples knows that usually gets me going in a big way. I always enjoy sex and foreplay with my husband. He is definitely and great lover.

While lying there in the bed, Kareem reached over and put his arms around me pulling me close to him. I responded immediately as to not give any indications I had been involved in a sexual relationship with another man. Kareem began his usually routine of foreplay; I played right into it. I was actually turned on by him. Kareem is a very sexy man. It's not that I don't find him attractive or sexy. I was just tired as hell from dealing with a beast of a man who is a damn sex machine. I felt Kareem's hard massive dick as he pull me even more closer to him. His dick was so hard it seemed I could feel it pulsating. Kareem's lovemaking styles was much difference from that of Styles. Kareem would often start slow and gentle, and gradually turn up the intensity. Styles would go for the gusto immediately for the most part. Sometimes he would really take his time, but Styles liked the fact of being in control, and dominant over his partner. It was a change, but I enjoyed it. Both Styles and Kareem have incredible stamina.

It really didn't matter how I was feeling, or what I was going through, I was not going to short Kareem my wifely duties because of my infidelity. He really didn't deserve that. I wasn't going to deny him, neither was I going to short change him in any regards. I am woman enough to know that he was away on business and not somewhere running the streets. He has proven to be a gentleman to me and a damn good father to our children. Although my body was worn the hell out, I was not about to come up with some lame-ass excuse about why I cannot perform. I love Kareem. I am going to do what I need to do, and I'm going to do it well.

I knew I was in for a treat. My nipples were still sore from Styles sucking the hell out of them like there was no tomorrow. My pussy was sore, and my legs and back were sore as well from all the positions he put me in. I thought that one time Styles were confusing me with a licorice stick the way he twisted and turned my body to his satisfaction. I keep having these flashbacks now asking myself, what have I gotten myself into?

During the course of making love to Kareem on his first night home, I could tell he was overly physical and dominant. He made the statement, "Damn baby, this pussy is hot, wet and open." I flinched, but he damn sho didn't know it. I thought to myself, hot, yes, wet, yes, but open, damn! I really don't know how to handle that. I'm like I'm fucked! I can't fool this man! What made him say that? Does he know anything? Shit! But I quickly recovered and said, "Baby, I miss you so much, until my body was calling for you. The minute you stuck your dick in me, I came. My pussy is just that hot for you. I thought about you every nice and day baby while you were away."

"Oh Nicole, I love you too baby! The dick good to you baby?"

"Yes! I love your dick baby! I love the way you love me Kareem."

Kareem and I continued to make love for over an hour. However, at times it seemed to me an eternity. This man is a sex machine just like Mr. Styles. I don't know where he gets his energy to perform like this, but he is a beast in bed! I don't know how much more I can take considering my precious activity.

Afterwards, Kareem and I both showered. We sat on the side of the bed just talking about everyday stuff. We talked about our past week experience and started to plan something for the next two weeks. Little did I know Kareem was feeling a lil guilty. He grabbed me and held me close to him only to tell me he had another conference planned in two weeks. This time like the other, it would be for a week. I was disappointed, but I understood the responsibility and demands doctors have in their profession. As always, I was supportive and understanding.

Damn, What the fuck is going on? I have to call Tamera! I have to fill her in on what is going on. I haven't really had a chance to check on her lately, but I got to touch base with her. I have to fill her in on everything. She is going to be blown away.

There is no way Tam is going go to believe what this girl has experienced lately. Fucking two men with anaconda-sized dicks, I must say, it's been an interesting week to say the least.

Styles was out early this morning jogging and doing his workout routine. Kareem had already left for work at the office. I glanced over towards Styles' residence and he was working out in the front yard again like deja vu. He was shirtless and wearing those black spandex workout pants. The first thing I noticed was that big thirteen-and-a-half-inch dick piled up in the front like a captured python snake. His perfectly shaped bubble ass was an advertisement in the newspaper. I couldn't think of anything but the way that man took complete control of me and fucked me until times got better or worse. Hell, at this point, who knows?

He noticed I was watching him from across the street. It was my perception he begin stretching, flexing, moving his body in a very seductive way. I was hot in the pussy all over again. I simply could not take this man putting of a private sex show for me. I was already in a perplex state of mind. I really didn't know what I was doing. I didn't know anything anymore. Styles decided to stop for a break before resuming a more rigorous exercise routine. After a jumping and running-in-place routine, he sat on the steps with his body facing me. He obviously had his legs gapped wide open. I could see that dick again. It was as if it was waving to me from across the street saying, "Come here Nicole." I still could not come to grips with how well built this man is. He is the most perfectly shaped human I have ever seen.

In my mind, I'm like, "What's a woman to do in a situation like this?" I walked to the curb to retrieve my mail, and Styles took this opportunity to speak and invite me over. I returned the morning greeting; however, I did not go over. He ask me if it would be possible to see him sometime soon. However, I did not reply directly, but I did say to him I had to organize and prepare something for Kareem's conference that is scheduled for next week. But for now, Mr. Styles, Kareem is home.

I made it known to Styles that Kareem has another conference he must attend next week, and I have to make sure things are in order for him. You could see each of those pearly white teeth in Styles' mouth as he expressed joy and excitement knowing we would have time to spend together again. I could see his dick move around when he discovered the possibility of us fucking again. In fact, to be quite honest, when I mentioned to Styles that Kareem would be out of town again, his dick instantly stood to attention. Just before he returned to his workout routine, he made a statement, "Cole, it's unfortunate you will be home alone again. Don't worry baby, I will definitely be your bodyguard. I will protect you from the wolves. I'll see you later Cole."

"Okay Styles."

"Hey baby, before you go. I want you to know, I really enjoyed the sex with you! It was exciting!"

"Styles!"

"No baby, I'm serious! I been thinking about it ever since you left. This time Cole, I going to take you to another level. Styles! Quit it! Baby, I'm dead serious! Listen bae, I'm going to give you an experience of a lifetime. Like your boy Simone De said, 'Give em something to talk about.' I'm going to show you how to tap into a sexual mental state that will blow you away. I assure you Cole, you're going to explode with ecstasy!"

The innocence of Nicole is now a thing of the past. More importantly, it never leaves the back of her mind that she is a dedicated mother. Her love for her children is genuine. Her love for her husband is also unquestionable. However, Nicole finds herself in a predicament that she is not sure she can sustain for any length of time. It's apparent she trapped between two worlds. Unable to withdraw from either further complicates things for Nicole.

From time to time Nicole would vacillate mentally between "should I follow my desire to entertain company with Styles?" and "should I remain home and be the perfect wife to my husband and ignore the inner force that pulls at me constantly for Styles?" Of course, I know the answer without a doubt. It's just sometimes you want to follow you heart instead of your soul.

Kareem will be leaving tomorrow. Is he expecting me to make love to him tonight? If so, I'm going to make that happen. However, if he makes no attempt at fucking tonight, I'm definitely not going to initiate anything. On the other hand, I'm wondering about Styles' statement he made earlier. He proposed to take me to a place sexually, somewhere I've never gone before. Although it sound exciting and interesting. I am not sure mentally I can handle going to that place. In fact, I'm not sure I can go to any place with Styles again. I am all confused.

Here he comes across the street on my side. He's not in my yard, but he's passing by on the sidewalk.

"Hello Styles!"

"Hi Nicole. It's good to see you Cole."

"You too Mr. Styles!"

"Where does this 'mister' business come from?"

"Well, I'm just showing respect to my elders."

"Yeah right, so funny! He hehehe! Is the coast clear?"

"Not yet. Kareem went to the office. He's not home at the moment. Okay then. I hope you thought about what I said to you. I'm going to take you a place sexually you have never even imagine. I know your pussy is wet right now Nicole. I know you're hot and wanting to fuck.

Look at my dick. Look at hard it is. I would love to fuck you right here tonight. I can't hardly wait! I have really been missing you Cole."

"Oh Styles, I've missed you too. We have to wait because if I fucked you tonight, your husband would surely know that you are fucking another man. I just feel like I would penetrate your hole and leave you wide open tonight."

"Stop Styles!"

"Answer me before you leave. Is that pussy dripping wet?"

"Yes Styles! It's really dripping wet."

I think it's time for me to stop and catch my girl Tamera up on all the shiggidy that's been happening. Tam will never believe what has transpired since I last talked to her. Damn, it's like I don't even know where to begin. This has been such an experience for me till I am still in disbelief. It's like now, I'm just riding the waves and enjoying the surf. I realize it can't last forever, therefore I feel the need to enjoy it while I can. I don't believe it's something I'll ever get involved with again. It's like an addicting drug; some drugs are highly addictive and others are not so highly addictive. In the case of Styles, It's obvious, he's highly addictive. Therefore, it is best not to tempt fate and take that first try. For many people, it was the first try that caused them to be hooked on a substance that tends to be much more powerful then they themselves.

So here I am, going by to check on my girl Tam. I have to look her in the face while giving her the 411 on all this shit.

"Tam girl, where are you? Tam! Tamera, where are you girl?"

"Hi Nicole! Oh what a pleasant surprise! I'm glad to see you! Come on in Cole! How have things been girl? You know I'm here almost each day in this boutique selling my butt off. Cole, I got to tell you girl, I never stopped thinking about your situation since you were last here. I didn't call because I felt you needed some time to work through it all. But that thing we call prayer, honey, I have prayed for you! Girl, for real Cole, I have prayed for you! He hehehe!"

"Oh shut up Tam. Girl, you know I have been very busy."

"Yeah, I bet you have!"

"Tam, girl, how was your trip? I remembered you told me you were traveling soon. I thought about you honey. I knew you were probably living it up in some fancy five-star hotel with a big fine hunk of a man at your side. By the way, did you have a date girl?"

"Well I had a lil sum, sum."

"You know we have to do our girl talk. Shit, five days!"

"Yeah it really wasn't that bad girl."

"Tam sit down girl. I have some real girl talk! When I came by the other day to see you, I was between thoughts. Should I or should I not. Well, I kinda let myself experience some things that you may say is out of character for me. I have been spending time with Styles, and we have established quite a friendship."

"Really girl!"

"Yeah! I mean quite a friendship. Kareem came home the other day. I was so glad to have him home girl. I really love my husband. He is one incredible guy! He just informed me that he is scheduled to be in California next week for six days. So, I'm like, what? Sister, let me give you the low-down on what's been happening! Girl! I really don't know where to start, so I'm just gonna start! Honey, you my girl Tam, you know I got to trust you a hell of a lot! Girl, you can't mention this to no one! Tam, girl, this is strictly confidentially. Honey, Mr. Styles, girl, is no joke! Tam, that man is a beast! I hate to say it like that! He is a masculine, dominant, robust romanticist. He know what it take to make a woman melt! Honey, Tam, I can't believe how this man has taken full control of our situation. He is a master of tapping into a woman's mental state. Most people hold their fantasy close to their heart. But this man was able to crack the code. When he is done, he will see to it that you are feeling totally uninhibited, complete, fulfilled, and fucking worn the fuck out! Really, I did not intend to have sex with this man. I was thinking more about maybe flirting with him to see how far I could go with it without crossing the line. I was set to flirt, entice, or maybe just do what I could to turn him on. However, when the moment presented itself, it was as if I could not say no!"

"Nicole girl, I have seen you in many situations, but in every one of them girl, you were definitely in control!"

"Let's just say Tam, Mr. Styles is a real alpha male! Girl, this man has stimulated me mentally, physically, totally everything! I mean e-v-e-r-y-t-h-i-n-g Tam! I melted under the spell of his big brown eyes, his masculine male voice, his broad buffed chest, his perfectly shaped ass, his massive thighs, his strong chiseled arms, his beautiful white teeth, long beautiful sexy dreads, and not to mention that big monster-size anaconda of a dick he has. Tam, I cannot stress how much this man has, girl just lit my fire. I mean lit my fire! When he touched me, immediately I wanted to fuck! Just with a touch from this man! I wanted to immediately just in the bed or somewhere and fuck this man like there was no tomorrow. Tam! Just a mere touch! Can you believe it! No foreplay, no caressing, just one touch! I was ready to drop my drawers or maybe even maybe just have him tear them straight off me. Whatever, I was ready! He gave me a friendly hug and I almost lost my damn mind!"

"Nicole, Girl, I can't believe this shit! Honey this man has cast a spell on you! He is simply incredible I see. Girl you are a mess!"

"Well, Tam, not really a mess. I just kinda out there right now. I'm gonna deal with it. But it's just that it really feel so good. Tam, he grabbed me and began kissing me so passionately. He buried his tongue deep in my mouth. Slowly he began licking my neck and ears. I just absolutely gave up. I did not try in any manner to resist. I stared him back in his eyes, and I literally went limp. I mean I did, I gave in to him! Girl, we ended up having sex, making love, rough fucking, whatever! I just know we were going at it with great intensity. I mean we has such chemistry, and I guess animal magnetism like you could never imagine! All I know is this man fucked the damn hell of me! Tam I told you he is super abnormal down there. He wasted no time sticking that monster of a dick deep inside of me and made damn sure I got every inch of it! Every inch of it!

"There were times I tried like hell to get away from that cock! But each time I move, he was right on me! I tried my all. I mean I tried to muster up all of my strength. Yet I was no match for Mr. Styles! He knew my weak spots. He knew exactly what turns me on, so he took advantage on it and used it to his good. Girl that man fucked me in every position imaginable! I had to ride that big monster dick for twenty minutes.

"He flipped me over on my back and threw my legs over my head and made damn sure they were spread as far apart as they could possibly be. He rose to a position of standing up in the bed horizontally while fucking me. He put pressure on the crease of my legs where they bend, which in turn caused my ass to rise towards the ceiling and he literally stood up in my pussy and wore me out completely! I nearly passed the fuck out, or maybe I did.

"He then pulled me to the edge of the bed on the corner and he stood straddle and worked on me for quite some time. I begged for a moment of relief. I needed rest! I need a break in the action. I mean my pussy was wet! My body was shaking like a leaf on a tree. I could not stop. I was at his mercy. We stopped for about five minutes and immediately kicked right back into overdrive. We fucked on the floor, on the washing machine, in each room of the house until there were no more.

"It was constant excitement! Each time he would stick his massive dick in me I would cringe! I would grab whatever part of his body and take a deep breath just trying my best to take it. To say Styles was a dominant fuck would be an understatement! This man held me down, and fucked me down. It looks like this girl, come hell or high water, it looks like this girl was going down! He hehehe!

"We end up going back in the bedroom and he gently laid me back on the bed and began sucking my nipples like an animal while all the time staring me right in the eyes. He slowly maneuvered his body so that his dick would line up with my wet pussy and before I knew it. He had slowly but steadily driven every inch inside me all over again. He worked it in and out, round and around, long stroke, short strokes and about five strong thrusts until he had me open like the Suez Canal honey."

"Cole no girl!"

"Honey yessssss Tam! Kissing me on my neck and sticking his tongue in my ears what he knew to do to get me started all over again. I absolutely could not resist, Tam, I was in, it seemed over my head. But the thing is, I enjoyed the hell out of it! I make no qualms about it. The dick is so damn good!

"Tam this hunk turned me over, and laid me on my back. He composed himself for what would seem like a fucking of a lifetime. He positioned me on the bed just where he wanted me. Then he looked me in my eyes deeply, like you're about to get fucked be a real man. He took my legs at the base of my ankles and played them over my head and positioned his thirteen and a half dick in me and I felt every inch of it and it penetrated my hot wet pussy, gliding down the walls and causing my pussy to shoot pussy juice everywhere.

"This man stood up in me and fucked me, and fucked me and fucked me! I was a limp rag doll when he decided to turn up the heat. He grind that monster dick deeper and deeper inside of me. I could not control the powerful orgasm that continued one after the other. I encountered spasms after spasms. It was a moment I had never experienced before.

"It was at this time Styles began kissing me so erotically and dominantly, I completely gave in to him. I witnessed him stand on his toes and sturdy them in the bed as he began pounding and pounding me with such force the average woman could never endure. The more we fucked, the more I wanted to fuck! I was all in at this time. I was in for the long hall. I thought to myself, I'm gonna give him what he wants, since I have no choice to start with! The more he kissed me, the more I relaxed and gave up my entire body. I remember my body submitting to the moment! We were so chemically drawn to each other it was crazy! Styles looked me in my eyes and stated in a masculine commanding voice, 'This is the art of the deal! The thirteen-and-a-half-inch dick, plus my skills has caused me to master sex. I call it the art of the deal. I understand women who find me attractive, and think they want to kick it with me, but they don't really understand a real man when they see one.'

"We took a break after fucking for over an hour, and reaching climax after climax. He put me back in the same position and began to repeat the same thing over and over again! He arched his back and drove all thirteen and a half inches in me once again! Tam girl, I was in for more than I ever knew, but it seems as though I could do nothing to stop it. To tell the truth, I didn't want to stop it. I wanted more and more! This time Styles worked that dick like John Henry worked the steam drill. Like no one has ever worked it before. My pussy was exploding time and time again. The bed was wet with sweat, cum, and pussy juice. I could not think straight at this time. I was lost in the moment!

"Nicole, girl, how could you handle all that? He hehehe!"

"He hehehe, hell! Tam, girl, this man is a man by every stretch of the imagination. This man then, Tam, had the nerve to sit up straight in the bed, pulling me forward to sit on top on his massive supper hard dick! You would have thought he swallowed five Viagras and five X pills. Some kind of way he was able to maneuver by picking me up and carrying me over to the dresser where a bottle of Crown Royal sat. He picked it up and the both of us began to drink and drink. After about five minutes, the two of us felt invincible.

"Styles walked me back to the bad and there we went at it all over again! He ordered me to ride that dick as I wanted to. Well, he didn't really order me, it was all a part of the role playing that we found so fitting for what we wanted. He gave me specific directions on how he wanted me to ride that dick and I was to do as he commanded. I was told to sit on that dick and fold my legs backwards and ride it like Turner rode Trimble. He hehehe! Girl, I was in for more than I could ever imagine! There were times when I was told to ride it fast, and there other times I was told to ride it slowly. I was told to grind on it and then just ride it down to the base and then all the way up to the tip. Now I want you to remember Tam, the dick is thirteen and a half inches. So I had to position myself to grind down to the base and then all the way back up to the tip of it. He would say things to me like, 'Ride this dick! Ride this dick! That's right, grind it baby! I got you! I got you!' Although I felt that big monster inside of me, my mind was telling me that he had me. But it was only him controlling the situation. He would say to 'nut on this dick, nut on this dick! Come on baby, give the pussy up!' I mean he was very vocal in his control, and I fell for every bit of it. I knew we were in a role-play mode, but it was like letting out true feeling come out that had been shut up for quite some time.

"There were times I could feel his massive cock just pulsating inside of me. I could feel the huge veins that were protruding from the sides of it. However, every inch of that monster was wonderful. I really had never seen a dick so enormous before. That is why between he and I, I decide to call him Thirteen and a Half. Girl, Tamera, we were in complete ecstasy, and very uninhibited.

"After two and a half hours I was drained, and cum was all over us. He then picked me up, put my legs over his shoulders, and walked around the room with his dick inside of me fucking me as if I was nothing."

"Nicole, girl this is unbelievable!"

"Yes Tam, very unbelievable! Tam I wish I was through, but I'm not! This man Tam, sat in a chair and told me to come here. I literally started to beg him to stop, but at the same time, I was caught up! I mean, I really wanted it! I sat on top of him facing him with eye-to-eye contact. He said to me I'm just getting ready to fuck you on another level. I once again rode his dick for another forty-five minutes. It was his way of breaking me down in his alpha male dominant role. Finally, he picked me up and slowly kneeled on the rug in the bedroom and spread my legs as wide as I possibly could while laying on my stomach. He placed a pillow beneath my mid-section. He startled me with his fine-ass robust body and drove that big anaconda deep in me while he licked the back of my neck and licked me in my ears. I was his for the taking.

"Tam, girl he turned my face to him while hitting my pussy from the back and began kissing me deeper and deeper in my mouth. I could feel myself slowly but surely yielding completely to him. Honey, Tam, at this point, I was all in! I mean I belonged to Mr. Styles! I had reached a level of submission that when he began driving that dick in me, girl, that nigga literally drove me crazy! He was power driving me like John Henry, I told you. I'm not lying girl! Tam, this man is a trip! He kept telling me that he is the art of the deal!"

"Girl, Nicole, What's that? Tam that means he has mastered the art of sex, and basically, he controls it! We decided to take a few more drinks of Crown and girl he had the nerves to put Simone De 'Feel so good' in."

"Oh shit Cole, I know you went crazy then! I don't know it if was over Styles of Simone De, but I know that at that point, you were gone! He hehehe! Cole, girl! I don't know what to say! Were you all finished?"

"Hell no! Tam, this stud turned me back over on my back and got on top of me and began fucking me like there was no tomorrow! He had created a rhythmic motion to his fucking. He would drive it deep five times, and then do a circular motion five times. Once again, my body was exploding in ecstasy.

"I could not stop cummin. I screamed and screamed until I was literally hoarse. My voice was giving out! I body was giving out. My pussy was giving out! There were times I tried my best to wiggle from under him, but it was no use. He was solid. Just massive, all man! I could do nothing to escape this sexual beat down. I continued to muster all my strength and escape from under Styles, but girl, every time I moved he was right on me! Somehow, I was able to advance forward until I reached the head of the bed. Little did I know, that's all he wanted. I was locked in. He knew it! He held my legs over again and began working me over! He was driving dick like crazy! He was grinding like he had lost his mind! He was deep kissing me and licking my neck and turning me head to stick hick tongue in my ears. This man was a damn sex machine breathing! He sucked my nipples and licked my tits. He then pulled me all the way down, and straddled me and stuck that big monster of a dick in my mouth! I couldn't do anything but go alone with it. We were totally in another zone! He mouth-fucked me for what seemed like a lifetime. Tam, you wouldn't believe it girl!"

"Girl, how in the hell were you able to handle all of that Cole?"

"I don't know Tam! What I do know is that he laid that pipe on me good, in fact, damn good! Somehow girl, I enjoyed every moment of it!"

"Nicole, girl, what are you going to do?"

"What do you mean Tam?"

"Well, Cole, I really feel like it's more than just sex! I hear and have heard what you said. I know the chemistry is powerful, well, it's amazing!"

"I know I love my husband Tam! I really don't understand how I got here!"

"Oh Nicole girl, it's just a fling. Don't worry, it'll fizzle out. Like they always say, this too shall pass."

"Kareem is out of town for a week again. Styles is already aware and making plans."

"What! Girl, he hehehe! Cole girl, you are too much! Kareem will be fine I'm sure! He's emersed in this work. Girl, Cole have your fun honey! Have your fun while you can! I'm telling you, this will fizzle out!"

"I know right! I keep telling myself it will."

"Cole honey, like they say, ride him cowgirl, don't let him throw you down! He hehehe!"

"Oh stop Tam! Just stop it."

Nicole's inside thoughts on her marriage.

Everything is happening so fast, so out of character for me. How does a married woman, mother, and a respectful professional, get caught up in a love, sex romance when she has been faithful to a man for years. I guess the human side of longing, wanting, and fantasizing can get the best of anyone. I have to acknowledge I have a wonderful husband; in fact, a very sexy, handsome husband whom I love and adore. I feel blessed and fortunate to have Kareem in my life as my soul mate if there is such a thing as one. I would rather have no other man to be the father of my children. This man adores the ground that I walk on. He loves me with all of his heart, mind, and soul. The very air he breathe gives sustained life to the both of us. He is my rock! I can always depend on Kareem to be the loyal, faithful, and kind gentleman that he is.

"Tam, This man really loves his family and is devoted to all of us. He is the lover of my soul. I guess the problem is, the last few months, Kareem has been traveling more and more with his work and doing research with his medical team. It's to be expected, so I deal with him being gone away from home quite a bit. I guess what's different now is the increase of frequency of being gone a lot often. I do understand that being a doctor has its demands of family life. Kareem said they are involve with a new medical research initiative, and it can be quite grueling at times. Girl Tam, you know I had to take a short leave for my job to deal with so projects I been working on. So I guess that's why I tend to notice him being gone more now.

"I must admit, Tam, it has taken so time for me to adjust to him being gone a lot. It seems like the trips are a lot longer too girl. I guess the thing is, when he is away we really don't talk too often because he's either busy with the research team or resting for the next busy day. He is also involved in the planning of these conferences as well, so he pretty much has to be there. We don't Skype, email, text, and call as much. He is just too tired when he completes his day. I'm not saying I don't hear from him; it's just that things are a little different, that's all. He's involved in presentations and speaking engagements at any moment he has to be ready to present if they have a no-show on the agenda."

"Oh girl Cole, Kareem loves you and those children. You know things will revert back to normal once he returns home."

"Oh look it's Kareem texting."

"What he say Cole?"

"I miss you baby! I can't wait to see you! Things are going well here. I'm being honored tomorrow, and I didn't even know it. I will call you a little later. Love you!"

"See there girl. I told you! You have an awesome husband as you well know."

"Oh yes I know, even if you don't Miss Tam!"

"Oh girl Cole he hehehe! He said he's going to call me later tonight. I really miss my big head man. Tam girl, I'll get back with you sis."

Kareem calls Nicole from California.

Ring, ring, ring.

"Hello baby!"

"Hi Cole! I love and miss you honey!"

"Oh Kareem, I really miss you more baby. I can't wait till you're home. By the way, when are you coming home?"

"I should be home by Saturday morning baby. I'm usually the last one to leave. I have to make sure everything is taken care of."

"Oh baby, I really understand! When you are a successful doctor like yourself, you're in great demand. Baby, I clearly understand Kareem."

"What have you been up to? Oh the usual honey. A lil house work, paying a few bills, working on several projects with my job. I have all of your favorite socks, drawers, hehehe!"

"Nicole, you are so silly!"

"I do Kareem! I have everything all ready for you baby."

"Thank you sweetheart, daddy don't know what I would do without you! That's why, like the old classic soul tune says, 'You are the sunshine of my life, that's why I'll always be around you!'"

"Oh Kareem!"

"Yeah baby! 'Ain't no mountain high enough, ain't no valley low enough, ain't no river wide enough to keep me from loving you!' I love me Cole!"

"I love my King Kareem more! Kareem I really miss you baby! That's why I love you so much! Baby it seems like we're living life right along with the lyrics of great soul music. I think about Simone De's bad jam, 'Come and go with me!'"

"Yeah Cole, Simone De's jam, the words 'I can't see you with another, I can't be with no other, I shared it with your brother, I even told your mother.' That dude be on some real shit! He's a great relevant artist."

"Kareem, I want you home baby."

"I want to be home Cole. It won't be too long now baby. My flight is scheduled to leave Friday night bae. It's scheduled for 6:00 p.m. That was the only flight with a shorter layover."

"Okay dear. I just wanted to know. Do you need me to pick you up?"

"No bae, I have my car at the airport. I know, but you may be too tired to drive. If you need me to pick you up let me know."

"Okay Cole, I'm about to get some rest baby. I will hit you up tomorrow my love."

"Sure Kareem. I love you baby!"

"I love you too! Rest well Cole."

"Thank you baby."

Oh I guess I better get me some rest. I feel like I will have a long day tomorrow. Damn, my phone is ringing! Who is that? I bet that is Tam. I know I left her abruptly earlier, but my mind was on my man Kareem. Oh! It's Styles!

"Hi Styles!"

"Hello Nicole! I wanted to check on you to see how you are doing tonight."

"Oh thank you Styles! Really, I'm doing fine. I talked with Kareem earlier tonight and he's coming home Saturday morning. So I'm trying to get some things done before he gets home."

"I see. I understand baby. Are you lonely tonight?"

"Styles, I'm in bed! I've already taken my shower and climbed in bed. Oh that's funny. What? Well, I took my shower not too long ago myself. And I'm just laying here in bed listening to Simone De's jam 'Talk to Me Baby.'"

"Oh really."

"Yeah! I'm laying here thinking about you Cole. I'm lying flat on my back with my legs wide open with nothing on just thinking about you. My dick won't go down. In fact, it's pointing right at your window. I tried just letting it be, but the more I think about you, the harder it gets."

"Styles."

"Cole, Cole..."

"Yes Styles?"

"Reach over there and play with that pussy. Play with it. Put your fingers in it and open it up. I want you to rub it. That feels good to you, don't it?"

"Yeah!"

"Keep playing with it."

"I am. It's good Styles!"

"My dick is rock hard Cole."

"I hear you Styles."

"Listen to me Cole, Listen to me. Get up put on your housecoat and come across the street."

"Styles, I'm in bed."

"Listen to me baby, put on your housecoat and come across the street. You hear me?"

"Yeah. The door will be open. You know what to do. Come right on back here to the bedroom."

"Okay, I'll be there in about ten minutes, no, five. Okay Styles!"

A few minutes later...

"Hello Styles!"

"Hey baby. Take your housecoat off! Take a sip of that drink I fixed for you."

"What is it?"

"I got you Cole, Drink all of it. It's good. I had one before you came over. That's why my dick won't go down."

"Styles, what is it?"

"It's something I got from a friend of mine. It's supposed to make you feel damn good. It's doing the job right now baby. Here hit this."

"Styles..."

"Come on baby, hit this a few time. It'll make you feel good!"

Nicole started to feel good.

"Stand over there in front of the mirror. Spread your legs and play with that pussy! Dance for me. Come on put yourself into it. Turn around. Bend over for me. Turn back around again and face me. Spread your legs, play with that pussy. Walk slowly over here. Get on your knees! Suck my dick! Suck it! Look at me while you suck it! That's right, keep sucking it like that! Go all the way down on it! Choke on it! Suck it! Lick the head. Now kiss it and look at me while you do it. Suck it! That's right, you're doing good. Come here sit on this dick! Ride it.

"Oh Styles ..."

"Shhhhh! Don't talk! Just ride the dick until I tell you to stop. Do what I tell you to do. Grind on it! Harder! Harder! Grind faster! That's right!"

"Styles, I'm tired! Keep riding, Get up on your knees and ride it! My god! Styles, I can't yes you can ride it baby! Keep going, l got you! Come up to the head and go all the way back down. Ride that dick, baby! Kiss me! Come here."

"Oh Styles you're kissing my neck! Oh my god! You have your tongue in my ear. Oh Styles, I can't control myself! Fuck me! Fuck me Styles! Fuck me!"

Scream, scream!

"I'm cummin! I'm cummin! Styles!"

Scream!

"My god! I got you! Don't stop! Keep going! Lay on your back Nicole."

"I can't Styles!"

"Lay on your back baby. That's right I got you! Love it! Enjoy the dick!"

Immediately I felt Styles penetrate me with his massive dick. It was hard as ever, and it felt like it was bigger for some reason. I remember he had given me something to drink earlier. It gave me a rush like never before! He positioned himself on me and began to fuck me like there again was no tomorrow! I had experienced this with him before. However it just seemed like this time he was in it to win it. He looked at me and said, "Kareem is coming home soon, and I want to give you something to think about. I'm going to fuck you good tonight baby. In fact, I'm going to fuck this pussy till morning! Lay back!"

"Styles I can't take it no more!"

He started to kiss me deeper and deeper! I was so turned on until I gave way to him! I just felt myself yield completely to him. He went deeper and deeper inside of me. I began to fuck him back and enjoy everything he had for me! I had left my body. I was seemingly in another place. I remember reaching a climax like never before. Styles worked his mid-section like a machine! I grant you, Styles worked every muscle in his body and fucked me mercilessly! I began fucking him back! I told myself this is not me, so I fucked him and tried to drain his body like he had drained mine. That night we fucked each other over, and over again for hours and hours!

By early morning, after waking up around five o'clock. I got out of the bed. I felt totally exhausted. I was tired as hell! My body was drained. I looked at Styles as he continued to lay there while watching me get up. He begged for me to come over to where he was. I literally ran out of there! I thought to myself, "This man wants to fuck again this morning!"

When I turned to look at him after he called me, I saw that big monster dick begin to rise all over again. I knew that I wasn't having any part of that! I hurried home to get a shower and then a bath. I wanted to soak in a tub on water with alum so hopefully my body could rejuvenate before Kareem would get home.

I'll just sit here for an hour and try to try to get myself get prepared for my husband. This has been like a drug addiction! I have been totally engulfed in the situation. I am now left wondering how and if I'm able to escape. It's like a real force keep calling for me, and I fall like prey to the call of a wolf. I don't quite understand it, but I can say it's real.

Damn, I don't believe it! I hear a car outside! Let me see who that is, It's Kareem! He tricked me! I didn't expect him for a couple more days. Here he is driving up in the yard.

"Hey Nicole!"

"Hi baby! Kareem you're home! Welcome home baby! I'm so glad to see you Kareem!"

"Wow! I must have been gone too long this time because I have never receive this kind of welcome before."

"Oh Kareem stop!"

"Ha hahaha! I'm just kidding baby, Cole. I'm just glad to be home baby. Cole, I'm about to get a shower."

"Okay bae, I'll fix you some breakfast."

"Okay Cole, just something very light. Hmmn, what's that smell? I smell alum and vinegar."

"Oh baby, I been working out and walking and my body is exhausted."

"Okay Cole, let daddy get a shower then I'm going to doctor on you a bit. I been thinking about a few ways I can doctor on my girl. You know your boy is a specialist. So I'm home and ready to be Doctor Feel Good this morning! Come on baby, let's spend a lil time together. How about giving daddy a lil playtime. In fact, can you come over and doctor on me? My back, legs, and my nice, fine black ass, as you would say, can use a little massage right now. Here let daddy pour you a lil cocktail first."

"Awesome Kareem, that would be great!"

I have to play the role so that he won't suspect anything.

"Thank you Cole! Now come here sexy mama! Let daddy run my fingers through your hair. Baby, you are so beautiful to me. Turn around baby. I want to feel your sexy soft ass against my dick. I love the way you move that body from side to side. Each time you press that ass on my dick, it gets rock hard."

"Ah, Kareem, I love it when you kiss me on the back of my neck. I been really missing that! I always love the way you work that tongue up and down my neck until you reach my tender ears. You know that just drives me crazy! In fact baby, that shit gets me even hotter. Kareem, standing here in front of you with that hard dick pressing against my hot, wet pussy is totally exhilarating! Your kisses are warm and gentle. I love the way you tongue my ears baby. That shit just does something to me. In fact, I want to fuck! Kareem, we can wait baby!"

"No way! I miss you so much Cole."

"I know Kareem, welcome home daddy."

"Nicole, you are even more beautiful now, than ever. Here sweetheart, take this off. Here, let me help you. Let daddy take these clothes off my baby. Nicole, your body is calling me!"

"Kareem, you're picking me up!"

"Yeah baby, daddy is picking his baby up and taking you to the bedroom."

"Kareem, I really love you!"

"I really love you too Cole."

"I love the way you make me feel Kareem. Hmmmn, auh, oh baby, Kareem! Auh! Damn baby!"

"I'm sorry mama."

"Auh! Oh, damn, Kareem! Shit your dick must have grown since you been away! Damn! Auh! Kareem! Oh my god!"

"Come on Cole, you can take it baby."

"Whew! Your dick is so big Kareem."

"I know baby, but you're used to it now."

"Auh, my god! You have your tongue in my ears. It feels so good. Oh I love it Kareem. Fuck me baby! Please fuck me daddy. It feel so damn good Kareem!"

"Your pussy is so wet Nicole. It's so damn good Cole. Come here, I want you to sit on daddy's dick. Daddy want you to ride this dick."

"Okay baby, it's so deep in me, I can't take it!"

"Yes you can baby, just ride the dick for me. That's right, ride the dick baby. Keep riding the dick Cole."

"Oh Kareem! It's so deep in me! I love your dick baby! I love the way you make me feel. Fuck me daddy! Fuck me good daddy! I miss you Kareem. I really miss you baby."

"Come here Cole, lay on your back. Put your legs over my shoulders. Auh! Auh! Auh! Kareem, you're so deep inside of my pussy! Oh Kareem! Keep it right there! Keep it right there baby!"

Scream, scream, scream!

"Oh my god! Fuck me baby! I'm cummin Kareem! I'm cummin!"

Scream, scream, scream, scream!

"Give it up Cole! Give daddy that pussy! That's right give it all to me! Let yourself go baby! Let yourself go. I got you! I got you baby!"

"Oh Styles!"

"What? What did you say?"

"I said I like your style!"

Damn! How in the fuck did I let something like that happen? I damn sure can't let that shit happen again. Damn! How could I? My husband is fucking me, and I call out another man's name. Shit!

"Take this dick Cole! Take it baby! Daddy been missing mama! Open that pussy! I'm about to cum Cole! Damn!"

"Come on Kareem!"

"Damn Cole, I haven't exploded like that in a while. Shit! Whew! Baby, let's get a lil rest. Shit! That pussy was good. Let's get a lil rest. I got something I want to talk to you about."

"What is it baby?"

"Nawl, we can talk a lil later."

"Okay Kareem. We'll talk later. Here baby, lay in daddy's arms. I love you Cole."

"I love you too Kareem!"

Kareem tells Nicole He has another conference.

"Good morning Kareem!"

"Good morning Cole!"

"Did you sleep well Reem?"

"Yes baby, I did sleep well. I released a lot of pressure, and I sleep very well!"

"So did I Kareem. I sleep very well just knowing you're home again."

"Well, Cole come here and sit down."

"What's wrong baby?"

"Nothing is wrong Cole. It's just that I have one more conference. I know it's been hard on you. But this is the last one for a while."

"When is it Kareem?"

"It's next week. But I will have to leave out tomorrow."

"Kareem, you're going to wear yourself out! Oh honey Kareem."

"I know baby! This is the last one for a while baby, daddy promises. Let's go out and have breakfast Cole."

"Okay Kareem, I'll be ready in a few minutes."

I can't believe this! I really can't fucking believe this! This is totally unbelievable! But this is what's it's like being married to a doctor.

"Breakfast was great baby. I really enjoyed the pancakes Cole."

"Yeah! They were great. I like pancakes from Pancake House! Really, this is my favorite place for pancakes!"

After a long day out with Kareem, it is now time to organize a few things for his trip. He has to leave early in the morning. At least, this is the last time for a while. We both are about to get a shower and get some rest from a very busy day. We have to be back up in a few hours to get him to the airport. We both know the airport can be a total nightmare.

We're up early and all set to go. This time I am dropping Kareem off at the airport.

"Baby I'm ready to go."

"Okay Kareem I'm ready too."

Traveling early in the morning is not so bad since there are fewer cars on the road. One great fact is we don't live too far from the airport.

"We are already here!"

"Okay Cole, I love you baby! I will see you soon."

"Okay honey, Kareem I love you."

"Call me when you can."

"Okay Kareem! I will!"

Damn! Let me call Tamera. I know it's early, but she won't believe this. I got to fill my girl in. Kareem just left for Atlanta, Georgia. I can now fill my girl in on the latest. I thought about just going by to see her, but I think I will save that drive and give her a call. Maybe she and I can hook up later for girls' night out.

Ring, ring, ring!

"Hello Tam! Hi girl!"

"Oh hi Cole! Great hearing from you Cole!"

"Hey girl Tam, I hadn't had the opportunity to call you, so I'm reaching out to you this morning girl. I called you to share a lil girl talk with you! Kareem is out of town, now maybe you and I can catch up. All this shiggidy that's been happening is too much for any one girl to handle! Besides, it's great when you can share your deepest feelings with someone whom you trust and not have to worry if it will be repeated. Having that special person when things are more than you fathom can be overbearing at times. This shit is mounting! I'm now feeling the pressure. Not to mention my body, it's taking a licking but it's still ticking! He hehehe! When a woman's emotions are running high and her decision-making process is obscured for whatever reason, a trusted friend can provide that much needed support to help get you through. Tam you have always had and been a great listening ear for me, as I have been for you."

"Cole girl! I know you have had a lot on your place here lately. But I'm sure it's all going to work out just fine!"

"Tam girl I haven't told you the half! It's been crazy girl! It's been sex, sex, sex and more sex from Styles and Kareem. Girl both of them black stallions are ruin and both of them have stamina like wow! Tam, this shit has been nonstop. I really don't care if I see another dick for ten years! My pussy has gone through trauma. I mean honey Styles has beat this pussy crazy, then Kareem came home for a day basically and tried to make up for all the lost time with him being away. Girl, it's been unreal! My lil body has been bent, stretched, pulled, flexed, and folded more than a NFL football team. Tam, I really love my husband, and I really have developed feelings for Styles. It's like I want both, but that's not possible. I don't know what to do at this point. I'm mesmerized by Styles. He totally controls the situation. We do a lot of role playing, and he is definitely in charge. Kareem is not much different. He's a little more gentle and passionate during lovemaking. But that Styles, honey that stud is a beast!

"I have pondered over the fact that my marriage is safe and secure. However, lonely at times. I begin to fantasize over what is a fantasy and what is reality. Tam, girl, I fucked up so bad! While Kareem and I was having sex, I called out Styles' name. He looked at me in a strange way and said, 'What?' I said to him, 'I like your style Kareem.' Girl, I had to look myself in the mirror and say, 'You fool, how can you call another man's name when your own husband is fucking you!' I clearly called out Styles' name while Kareem was making love to me. He immediately picked up on it, but I quickly stated, 'Kareem, I like your style.' I'm not quite sure if he bought it or not. I think he did, but hell, sometimes, you never know!"

"Girl that shit was unreal! Just imagine if the show was on the other foot! You would be livid!"

"I know like hell I would! Well Tam, I better get back home now, my car in filthy and it's such a beautiful day. I think I'm going to wash it when I get home."

"Girl take that car and have it cleaned."

"I could, but I just like cleaning it myself. I'll just change into something more comfortable and get it done! Usually Kareem would keep it clean, but he's been traveling lately. But it's no problem at all."

Styles comes over after he sees that Kareem has left again.

I'll get my music going and wash her down. It's such a beautiful day! Let me put Simone De in. There it is. I want to hear "Bad Boy!" I have everything ready, and I'm at it listening to my boy! Oh my, look who's crossing the street!

"Hello Styles! How are you?"

"I'm great Cole, how are you? It's great to see you on this gorgeous day. You know I can get that done for you in no time."

"No, Styles. Thank you! But I got it!"

"Oh Cole! You wet me all up! Stop baby! Cole you're spraying water everywhere! Cole, ha hahahah! Okay I see how you want to play. Here let me see the hose. I will finish the car."

"Styles! He hehehe! Stop, you're wetting me all up! You're wetting my clothes and hair. Styles stop!"

"That's what I'm trying to do! I feel like if I get you all wet and shit, we can go inside and get a lil more comfortable, if you know what I mean."

"Don't even try it Mr. Styles!"

"Yeah baby! Getting you wet really turns me on. In fact, I love to get you all wet and hot at the same time. I would like to take you home tonight and show you a damn good time. If you let me, I will do some things to you that you probably hasn't had done before."

"Oh really?"

"Yes Nicole really!"

"What's that supposed to mean Styles?"

"Well, you just have to agree to give me the opportunity to show you what I'm talking about."

"Well maybe another time Styles."

"Cole, baby the night is perfect. I can feel your energy baby. I will take you places we've or you've never gone before."

"Styles!"

"Bae, just say yes."

"Well, maybe."

"I guess I'll have to take that for now since we're still cleaning your ride. I figure by the time we're finished, you can come over to my place and get a shower, then we can *laissez le bon ton roulette,* let the good times roll!"

"Oh Styles! You're just so full of yourself!"

"Nawl baby, I just want to make you feel good that's all! I got you! I have some things very special for you! I have been thinking about something, now it's just the fact of making it happen. I'm damn ready! I believe you're ready as well! Come on baby, Let me get your boy Simone De to help me, especially when he says, 'Come and go with me!' Bamm! Ha hahaha!"

"Ha hahaha my foot Mr. Styles!"

"Look at me girl. I got you! Plus I don't know how long Kareem will be gone this time, but something tells me it won't be as long as usual. You have probably laid down the law to him. So we got to make the best of our situation for this to go around. Is it another medical conference or damn is it a chick somewhere?"

"Don't you even go there Styles! I don't play that shit! Now you're going too far!"

"Hey baby . . ."

"Hey baby my ass! I don't play that shit."

"Okay! Cole you made your point! I'm so sorry. I didn't mean it. Wait a minute Cole. Let me finish the car, and you just stand by and let me know if I miss something. How about that? Hello?"

"What the fuck ever!"

"Damn Cole! Is it like that? Damn girl, I really pissed you the fuck off."

"Yeah, and you bout to make me kick your ass!"

"Hold on now, wait a minute, now, I don't know how much ass you're gonna be kicking, but not here young lady."

"Fuck you!"

"Damn girl! But I'll take that Cole, for now. May I ask you a question?"

"You may ask me a question Styles."

"How long will Kareem be away this time?"

"Well he texted me earlier and said it will be two weeks or a lil less. This will be the last conference for the year. At least this will be the last full traveling conference."

"So you have the house to yourself."

"Yes, my daughter Tia is away on a retreat."

"Oh, I didn't know you had a daughter. Yes, she's sixteen! She is a very bright young lady. She's also a daddy's girl by every stretch of the imagination."

"I bet! So when are you expecting Ms. Tia?"

"She is actually scheduled to return home on Friday."

"Oh well, we still have plenty of time to explore the essence of what makes your fine sexy body overly stimulate a man like me."

"Oh please!"

"I'm dead serious bae. When I think about you at night, my dick instantly becomes rock hard."

"Styles, you need to stop!"

"I'm serious Cole. Baby, when I think about you and all the sex we have had, I get an instant hard like fuck! My dick starts to pulsate constantly! You lights my fire Nicole! Do you hear me girl? You really lights my fire. The other day, I was outside doing my morning routine workout, of course I had on my spandex workout pants. Baby, if someone would have passed by, I would have been so fucking embarrassed."

"Why?"

"Cole, shit, my dick was super hard and would not go down! It was like, 'I want to fuck Cole right now without any room for negotiations.'"

"Okay Styles."

"Interesting enough while I was working out, a cute lil Latino chick passed by in a bad-ass black Camaro and saw me and instantly hit her breaks and backed her car just to speak to me."

"Oh really!"

"Yeah bae, she was bad. I shot the shit with her for about five minutes."

"Did you get that bitch's number?"

"Yeah, she gave me her number."

"What did you do with it?"

"I have it in my wallet."

"Give it to me right now!"

"Why?"

"I want that damn number Styles."

"Okay baby, it doesn't mean anything to me. I just took it because she offered it to me."

"Yeah fucking right! I see you didn't have any problem taking it! What did that bitch say to you?"

"Oh, she just complimented me on my body. She said I was the finest guy she had ever seen. She said my muscles were so defined and sexy. She told me to turn around."

"Why did that bitch do all of that?"

"I guess, she wanted to see my ass. She ask me if she could touch it. I told her she could."

"Oh really!"

"Yeah, it's no big deal. Come here girl. I want you! I got you Cole! I'm not interested in her."

"Yeah. Did she feel on your dick?"

"Well, she did not feel on it, but she wanted to see it, the print that is."

"What did she have to say?"

"Well, she thought it was the biggest she had ever seen."

"Then what did she do? Is that when you got her number?"

"Well, actually yes! Well, Cole, sweetheart, what are we going to do with this very welcome window of time?"

"Styles, what do you mean?"

"Well, hubby is out of town! Tia is out of town, and your son, he's out of town. Nicole, listen, I have great feelings for you! I have really enjoyed spending time with you. I really want to expand on that tonight! I told you, your sex is the best! I have enjoyed every minute of putting this dick on you!"

"Styles! Be a gentleman!"

"I'm telling you the truth! I really like fucking you babe! The chemistry is awesome! You remember what I said to you the last time we were together."

"What's that Styles?"

"I said to you, 'The next time I put this dick on you, you are going to go insane!' Look at me Cole. What do you see?"

"What?"

"Really, what do you see?"

"I see a tall, well-built, handsome black man."

"Okay, my point exactly. You see a man, a real man! In fact, a real alpha man. That's what I am. That's what I will always be! I'm a woman pleaser, and I like to fuck. I can get into the making love kinda thing, but Styles likes to fuck! I have all the experience in the world when it comes to pleasing a woman. I watched all of your reactions the last time we had sex. I fed off all your moves, everything you did. I responded to you! You see it's never about me! It is just that I know exactly how to tap into a woman's intuition and energy give her exactly what she really wants and deserves. Each time you tried to escape the dick, I knew I had it planted deep inside of you. But you would wiggle and wiggle trying to run or move a way, but I wouldn't let you! I was right on you like white on rice. I was there baby girl grinding that pussy good. Daddy fucked you with a deep, passionate, dominant fuck. Do you know why? Hmmmn, Cole?"

"What?"

"Do you know why I fucked you so good baby? It's because I knew you really wanted it and needed it. So that's why daddy would play in that pussy all night or all day until I got tired. Damn bae, it's getting dark out here and we still talking! I guess we're having another kind of sex right now. We just can't get enough of each other. I bet that pussy is soaking wet right now."

"Stop Styles!"

"Stop Styles. Ha hahaha!"

"That's not funny Styles."

"Oh come on baby, take a joke sometimes! I'm going to the crib Cole. I will see you in about fifteen minutes."

"Hmmmn..."

"Okay now Cole! That black Camaro make come back through here."

"Fine Styles! Let the bitch roll back through here! Help yourself Mr. Everything to all women!

Nicole comes back over again.

"Hey sexy mama! I like the way you look tonight bae! You are one sexy ass woman! Everything is in the right place on you. Damn! Come here, Kiss me. Hmmmn. Here baby I fixed you a drink. I think you are going to love this! I mixed a Red Bull with some of my special ingredients. It's gonna make you feel damn good in a minute. In fact, you gonna feel like Wonder Woman in a few minutes. Let me put on some great music for you. I got your boy Simone De. I got that jam 'Let's Do It Again.' He jams the hell out of that. How are you feeling baby?"

"I'm feeling good."

"Yeah, I bet you are! Come to daddy. Let me hold you girl."

"Oh Styles, you kissing me on my neck! Auh! You kissing me in my ear! Oh Styles! Auh! Oh baby, Styles. I'm feeling so damn good!"

"Kiss me Nicole. Stick that tongue all the way down my throat! Since you're feeling so good. I want you to take control for a while tonight. He let me take off your clothes. That's right Cole, take off daddy's clothes. That's right mamma! Go on down on that dick! Put it where you want it! Suck on it then! That's right, look at me while you suck that dick. Make love to that dick! It's yours. Show me what you got! Look at me while you're sucking that big dick. Lick my balls. Yeah! You got it bae. Lick them balls good. Put both balls in your mouth! Now, put that dick back in your mouth. Damn girl you're hot tonight. That shit got you feeling good don't it? You feel good, yes? I know it. Come here, I got you in the air. Taking you to me bed. But before we get in the bed, we're gonna use the floor. I'm gonna floor fuck this pussy tonight! Lay here on the pallet baby. That's right, kiss me! Shit you're turned on!"

"Oh Styles! Auh! Oh, you drive me crazy when you kiss my neck and ears! You make me want to fuck."

"That's what I want you to do!"

"Oh Styles, you sucking my nipples so good! I feel so good Styles! Keep sucking my nipples Styles. Please Styles, I want to fuck! Auuuh! Dammmn! Shit! Your dick is so big going in my pussy! Oh, Styles, you are fucking me so well! Give it to me please! Styles I love it! Please fuck me harder! My god!"

"Give it up Cole! I got you babe! Give the pussy up baby girl! Open your legs all the way! Let daddy fuck this pussy tonight for you!"

"Styles, yeah babe, you got my legs all the way over my head."

"I know just take the dick! Scream! I like to hear you scream Cole. I can't help it Styles!"

Scream, scream, scream, scream, scream!

"Auh! Fuck! Styles! Styles!"

"Baby, Cole you digging your nail in my back baby."

"I can't help it!"

"Turn over Cole lay on your stomach. I'm gonna fuck this pussy from behind! Shit Cole, I'm about to cum. This pussy is so good! Oh you can't run! You can't run. I'm gonna be right on you. Everywhere you move, I'm gonna be right on you! Spread your legs. You feel that dick?"

"Yeah!"

"You feel it?"

"Yeah!"

"Take this dick! Take it! Don't pass out on me. I'm just getting started! Get on your knees! Arch that back! That's right. Arch that back. Keep it right there! Right there! Don't move, keep that pussy right there! Damn this pussy is wet! Turn over and sit on this dick. I'm gonna tear this pussy up right here on the floor. Ride this dick! Ride it! Keep riding it bae! Don't pass out on me! Grind on this dick! This is your dick fuck it! It's your dick, fuck it! Come here, suck this dick. Choke on this dick! Make love to the head of this dick for me. Make love to this dick! When I touch your breast, and gently rub my hand up and down each one of them I can feel how hard they are. You are turned on like hell Nicole. Your pussy is soaking wet. I made you a promise that I was going to fuck you good tonight, and I'm going to do just that. I'm gonna fuck this pussy physically and your mind mentally. Get to the edge of the bed baby. That's right, that's where I want it!"

"Oh Styles! You're killing me! You're killing my pussy Styles! Your dick is so big, my god! Oh my god! Oh my god! I'm cummin! I'm cummin!"

Nicole's phone is ringing.

"Oh my Styles, I'm out of breath! Whew! You know how to completely drain a woman's body."

"Auh baby, what you think about yourself? You are simply amazing in bed Cole. You are such a beautiful, classy woman. I wish you were all mine. But, I'm definitely willing to share you with Kareem. Ha hahaha!"

"Don't even try that shit Sir!"

"You know I'm just kidding Cole. I know how uptight you get when it comes to Kareem. He is such a lucky and blessed man to have you."

"Is that my phone ringing? Yes that's my phone. Please excuse me for a minute Styles. Maybe this is Tamera. I have been trying to contact her for a few hours. I think her phone has been acting up lately. No, this is not Tam, this is Susan my accountant. Hi Sue!"

"Hello Nicole, I'm just completing a monthly analysis on your special account expenditures. I have a few questions. I know it a lil later than usual. Okay, I can answer them now. I was wondering if maybe you could come by the office in the next couple of days to discuss a few things. Sure, that's not a problem. Thank you Nicole, just give me a call and let me know you're in route. Sure thing Sue! I'll talk with you later!"

I just think it's so strange, I haven't heard anything from Tamera. I have called and left several messages. Let me try her Facebook page. Oh, she's on there now! I will send her a message.

"Hello Tam, girl you know you have to stay in touch with me! I have some hot and heavy talk for you! Let me know when you have time to sit and chat about a few things honey."

Oh, my! I see Tam is out of town. She didn't tell me she was going out of town! I see her GPS Locator is indicating she is in Atlanta, Georgia. She's close to where Kareem is staying.

"Cole . . ."

"Yes Styles, come on over here girl."

"I'm coming."

"No, you're not really cummin right now. You were a few minutes ago."

"Oh stop big head Styles! Just quit."

"Okay babe, I got you."

That's kind of strange. Usually when Tam is going out of town, she would reach out to me and let me know! She probably had to attend one her clothing markets for the boutique.

"Thank you Styles for assisting me in cleaning my car."

"You are more than welcome! Look at the big payoff I received as a payment. You gave me all kinds of benefits. I think I received triple pay today! Damn, if the pay is that good, when is the next time I can clean your ride and get a pay like the one I received tonight."

"Actually, Kareem will be back soon, and I am eager to put all of that back in his hands. But don't get it twisted Mr. Styles. I had already cleaned the car over eighty-five percent before you ever showed up to assist me."

"Eighty-five percent? Girl you must be kind of delusional right now. I think you may have contributed about forty percent."

"Whatever! Styles, I'm the one who did all the washing, wiping, and drying! The only thing you did was take out the trash, and wiped the seats off. So you need to just stop Mr. Styles!"

"Oh my, I love the way you say stop! It reminds me when we were on the floor and you were trying to push me off of you. Although it was just a sham. I knew you didn't want me off of you. I quickly overpowered you by kissing you nice and slow. I stuck my long tongue down your throat, ha hahaha."

"Oh so you think that shit is funny do you Mr. Styles?"

"Not really Cole. I just had a flashback."

"Yeah I bet! I thought about when you came in and I began taking your clothes off how sexy and fine you were. My dick stood to attention immediately! I was standing there in my black sexy drawers and it literally drove you crazy! I could see your nipple began to harden and I could tell at that point that pussy was hotter than a firecracker. I observed your eyes affixed on my dick as if you wanted to eat it, suck it, or fuck it! I just know you wanted to do something with it. I had prepared you a nice cocktail to get you ready for a big cock in your tail."

"You're crazy Styles!"

"No, think back babe. While I was standing there. My thirteen-and-a-half manhood was already rock hard damn near as soon as you entered the house. I offered you a nice drink and I watched you slowly drink it. In about five minutes you had taken this dick in your hands and was slowly massaging it. I didn't waste any time pulling you close to me, as I began to kiss you so erotic and passionately.

"Then, as you began to get hotter and hotter, our eyes locked and it was as if you knew to go down and start licking and sucking on the big anaconda. Each time you put your beautiful sexy lips around my dick head, and begin sucking it. I would take the palm of my hand, and place it on your head and slowly push your head down on that dick until I heard you begin to choke. I must admit, you have really come a long way at sucking my dick than when we first got started. In fact, I think you are a master at it now!"

"Fuck you Styles!"

"Come on bae! I'm just saying, I think you have it now. I can't lie bae, you are damn good at it!"

"Styles, I'm about to cross this street and go home."

"Okay sweetheart, I may call you back a lil later."

"I don't think so brother."

"Ha hahaha! Well, alright Cole. I am about to take a shower and get myself together."

Ring, ring, ring!

Damn, my phone is ringing again. It may be Kareem or Tam. It's Kareem!

"Hello bae!"

"Hi Cole! I love you my sweetie Cole."

"I love you more my honeybun Kareem. How are things going at the conference?"

"Things are going great Cole. Everyone is very impressed with all the details and organizing that went into planning the event. In fact, my lead coordinator who is over several hospitals had me to stand before the entire attendees for doing a great job in pulling things together in such a short notice."

"Oh Kareem, that's wonderful! I am so proud of you!"

"Thank you Cole! I really appreciate you bae. You know my motto. If you gone do it, do it right."

"I know Kareem. I know Mr. Perfect. It has to be right for you, and that's the way it should be."

"So tell me Nicole, what have you been up to?"

"Well, you know, the usual. I'm getting a lot of things done in the house. Also, in my downtime, I have been listening to The Bad boy Gentleman of Soul, Simone De. You know he's my favorite guy! He has a new CD out, and it's smoking hot!"

"Oh really, I will have to pick up a copy and check it out."

"Oh please do. The title is 'Unbelievable,' and he has his first gospel CD out as well entitled 'Heaven Help Us Please.' They did an outstanding job with both of them. You know I love listening to my music at night after I settle down. I usually light a couple of candles, dim the lights, and listen to my boy. I just love his music. It reminds me of the great soul music of the '70s and '80s. He has this gospel overture and a hoarseness to his voice that makes it magical. Sometimes I'll grab a glass of wine and just kick back."

"I got you baby. Well, I know you love your music. I want you to enjoy every minute of it. I want you to know I am going to make this leaving and disappearing up to you real soon."

"Okay Kareem. It's nothing baby. I really understand it's what you do. So I really understand!"

"Have you talked to Tia?"

"Yes, she is having a ball! She should be home in a few days."

"That's great! May be we can all go out for dinner when I get home. We could use that time to catch up on some family time."

"That sounds great Kareem!"

"Okay Nicole, I better get back and make sure things are going well."

"All right honey, I love you Kareem!"

"I love you more Cole. Bye bye."

Nicole tries calling Tamera again.

Ring ring ring!

"Hello? Oh, hi Nicole!"

"Hey girl. I have been calling you for some time now!"

"I am so sorry Cole. My phone service acts a lil crazy at times. I been having trouble with this phone honey not receiving calls, dropping calls, and not letting calls go through."

"Really girl! Tam I knew it had to be something!"

"Nicole girl, I thought about you and Mr. Styles. This man is a real sex machine girl."

"Yes he is Tam. He is definitely that and more. I could have never imagine anything like this happening to me. You know me girl. That all-American faithful wife, mother, career woman, and friend."

"I know Cole. But the way you are expressing your feelings about this guy is far unlike anything I have ever heard from you."

"You know Tamera, I really love my husband and we're solid as a rock. I am feeling guilty for having an affair while Kareem is away. I just hate to say those words, and actually acknowledge this reality, but that's just what it is, reality. Tam, you know that goes against everything I believe in girl. Kareem is a damn good husband, father, doctor and just all around great man. I love his very much. I think I'm beginning to get lonely when he's away. It just so happen a fine black specimen of a man showed up in the right place at the right time, and I got caught up. After realizing all of this Tam, I still find it hard to believe I am here in this predicament."

"Oh Cole, don't beat up on yourself too much. Sometimes life takes up places we probably wouldn't choose to go. So sometimes, things just happen. I know exactly what you mean Cole. I have been in similar situations myself. We have to play the hand that is dealt to us to the best of our ability."

"Girl, Tam I'm strong. I'll get through it!"
"I know you will."
"Thank you Tamera! Girl where are you Tam?"
"Oh girl I'm in Atlanta, just a couple of blocks from where you said Kareem booked his hotel."
"Oh really! Girl I didn't know you had to go to Atlanta!"
"Yes Cole, I have buyer's meetings for my business."
"Oh, okay! Maybe you two will get a chance to meet up and have dinner or lunch."
"I don't know Cole. I'm quite busy girl. Besides, I know Kareem probably won't have time with his busy schedule. Has Tia made it home girl?"
"No not yet. She should be here in a couple of days."
"Oh, okay, I know she is having a ball."
"Yes she is! I spoke with her, and she is really enjoying herself."
"Cole girl tell me, are you really enjoying sex with Styles? I mean, I understand everything you've shared with me. I'm just wondering, have the flame gone out. He he he he!"

"Tam, I am having a great time with Styles! It is definitely something I have never experienced before. When I think I can call him and call it off, I find myself hanging up the phone because I really don't want to call it off. Tam, I am telling you, this man can tap into your deepest innermost fantasies and make you explode with ecstasy! He has this alpha male dominance about himself. He like to be completely in control."

"What?"

"Yes Tam! He has to be in total control. His sex is mentally as well as physically. You forget all about being a lady he hehehe! The real animalistic traits comes out. You simply allow it to happen in that moment. He pushes you beyond your conceived capabilities. He is incredible!"

"Nicole girl, I know you will stay on top of things, you always have."

"Oh, you better believe it! I will enjoy it while it lasts. I am definitely enjoying the moment and absolutely enjoying that dick he hehehe! Tam girl, to say he knows how to use it would be an understatement! Girl, Tam you remember when I told you how he fucked me for hours the other day? Girl I was sore for days! Tam, that's no lie. I was sore for days. I'm supposed to be seeing him later at his crib."

"Oh really!"

"Yes, he's talking about taking me somewhere sexual I've never been before. Now may I remind you Tam, this man has already fucked me in every possible position, in almost every room in his house. It's like, what's left? Girl, Tam, Kareem is a damn good lover as well! He is a sex machine himself! I ain't gone lie to you. Kareem can put some dick down girl."

"Really Cole!"

"Yeah! Honey, Kareem, I calls him my Doctor Feel Good! Tam honey, when that nigga came home, I was already trying to recover from the beat down I had received from Styles. Styles had fucked me almost inhumanely. I mean nonstop! Girl soon as Kareem got home, he wanted to fuck! I was like, 'Please Kareem, I'm fucked out! I couldn't take another dick that day if my life depended on it.' But my husband wanted to have sex, and I could not refuse him. Kareem and Styles are different in some ways and alike in others. Kareem has this pretty boy look yet masculine, and Styles has this alpha male, masculine, hard black look of a real, pure, thoroughbred dominant black alpha male.

Tamera sense Nicole is on to an affair with her and Kareem.

Now that bitch can't figure out that I am fucking her husband. Nicole, Nicole, Nicole, as I think to myself, we are friends, but all the things you've shared with me about how good your husband is, how good Kareem can fuck. I'm like damn, I'm about to see for myself! Now, I'm just thinking to myself, what am I supposed to do? She is telling me how well Kareem can eat pussy, how well he can slang that dick, how good he can make a woman feel. Shit! I'm like I can't take it no more! I got to check the goods out for myself! When a woman sit up and share all of her deepest innermost feelings with another woman, I suggest she look out. Because that woman is about to set her plan in place to find out all the details for herself. Shit, she was telling me all about Styles and how well he can fuck and serve that dick. Also how well Kareem can serve that dick as well. Shit, I became curious and wanted to find out myself.

Kareem and I have known each other for almost five years through my friendship with Nicole. Although I must admit, he is a fine-ass specimen of a man! I have always found him to be sexy, handsome, and intriguing. I always thought to myself if I had a man like that, I would sit back and wait on him hand and feet. His sexy baritone voice just lights my fire and turns me the fuck on! My pussy has dripped pussy juice every time I had the opportunity to be in his presence. I must admit, like Nicole said, he is definitely packing a humongous dick. I mean watching him walk just, damn, drives me crazy. He has this lil sexy sway when he struts his stuff. Man oh man, that dick is so big until I have fantasized many time about having it deep inside of me. Little does she know, I have already had Kareem, Dr. Feel Good.

I can attest that Kareem does know how to please a woman. So one night when I went to visit Nicole at her home, Kareem informed me that she had left for Birmingham to pick up some items she ordered for Tia's science project. It would be an overnight trip according to Kareem. This hunk of a man was sitting there in his boxes having a nightcap. He invited me to join in.

I accepted Kareem's invite and I entered inside and sat down for a quick chat. We shared conversations, likes, and personal interests. During the course of our conversation, I remembered Kareem had a beautiful candle lit, lights dimmed, and a cocktail in his hand. He kindly, being the gentleman he is, offered me a cocktail. I accepted and we toasted the night with a carpe diem, seize the day! We shared the night listening to Simone De's jam, "Tonight Is the Night." It was a wonderful mood between the two of us.

By now, Kareem was on his third cocktail, and I was on my second and feeling real good. The two of us, after listening to the music and feeling the moment, we began to slow dance and it quickly lead to hugging and kissing. We continued for quite some time and ultimately began having hot steamy sex that got wild and intense.

It's no secret. Kareem is a damn good lover. I mean the man knows how to lay some pipe, and he has plenty to lay. Damn I can concur, he is my doctor feel good! I know firsthand how good the dick is! I also know Kareem has mastered the art of eating pussy. That brother literally ate my lil ass up. I was screaming and hollering like someone was killing me! The more I screamed, the more he forced me back down and ate me like there was no tomorrow! Pleasing a woman's every sexual appetite is Kareem's forte. I mean he know exactly what to do!

I remembered when he laid me down on the floor the night we were just chilling. Man oh man, Kareem very passionate began kissing me, and he got more and more intense. He starting kissing me on my ears and on my neck. The both of us got hotter and hotter! He fucked me so deep. I could hardly keep up with him. It was like I had tapped out or something. Damn, I remember it went on for about three hours. The dick was amazing!

Nicole didn't realize when she shared the innermost things about Styles and Kareem, it intensified my interest and made me want him more and more. I was determined to see what all the hype was about; now I can say, he is one incredible man!

Nicole never realized my frequent visits to her home was due impart to see her and catch up on girly things, but the other reason was to see and build a relationship with Kareem. While there, sometimes Nicole would excuse herself and leave Kareem and me there together. We would just sit and laugh, and tell a few jokes as we somehow felt we were building something very special. We even started a touchy-feely kind of thing while laughing and playing. We allowed an unspoken type of bond or chemistry that gradually draw us closer together.

One evening I went by to visit Nicole, it was late evening. I didn't realize she had not made it in from work. However, Kareem being the perfect gentleman that he is invited me inside and offered me a drink. We sat and talked for over an hour. Not to mention, after drinking a few, we both were feeling pretty good from a rum on the rocks. Kareem began complimenting me on how well I looked. He was intrigued with my beautiful sexy eyes as he put it. Shortly afterwards, he ask me to stand up so that he could get a better look at who were the tallest out of the two of us. We both knew the real answer, obviously, Kareem was six feet tall and he literally dwarfed me. However, I wasted no time at the opportunity to stand directly in front of this fine specimen of a man. In fact, I was absolutely delighted!

Kareem reached out and gradually pulled me towards him. I could feel his dick against my back. I could feel the impulse each time as it grew harder and harder. He took his long arms and wrapped them around my waist. I could now feel the warmth of his body and the change of his breathing as he would lean forward and kissed me on my neck. Slowly, he would bite me on the back of my neck and stick his tongue in my ears. I could feel his energy as he began to slowly grind his dick against my ass with his humongous man tool. It was like wow! I could feel my body giving away to him. I felt myself going limp.

Tamera is with Kareem in the hotel in Atlanta, Georgia.

I turned toward Kareem and looked him deep into his piercing hazel brown eyes. I was convinced we were headed toward something that was much bigger than this moment. Kareem wasted no time in turning towards me with a look of lust, passion, and desperation! He stared me in my eyes. I felt like he was almost in a trance by the way he continued to stare without a blink. It was an amazing moment for the two of us. I could feel every fiber of his being. I could sense the energy that was flowing so magically and magnificently. I could tell this was going to be a moment to remember. I was more confident knowing it wasn't me, but this brother wanted to fuck tonight. As he continued to stare at me, he very passionately stated Tamera, I want to feel your body with every inch of my dick! We could hardly resist the urge to embrace and kiss each other with a fire and fiery none has ever known. I must say that Kareem was a very passionate kisser! My panties were wet, and obviously, my pussy was hot as a firecracker! I was ready to fuck this man. I really had no problem reciprocating his advances.

While I was getting ready to get it on with Kareem in Atlanta, to my surprise, I received a call from Nicole. That's right, while I was standing there with Kareem. I immediately asked to be excused and went into the ladies' room and greeted Nicole as I would at any other time.

"Hi Cole!"

"Hi Tam!"

"Girl, Nicole what are you up to?"

"Tam girl, I'm moving a lil slow because I had an encounter with Mr. Styles earlier today. He promised me the next time we got together he was going to take me around the world without leaving the room. I must say, he did not lie! Girl, Tam, you know we can't go too long without catching up with each other. By the way, I walked across the street in a very inconspicuous manner. Styles was waiting for me at the door. It was as if he planned a sexual, submissive, sadomasochism kinda shit!"

"What are you saying Cole?"

"Tam, girl I'm telling you, this nigga is a beast when it comes to sex! When I entered the house, there were drinks he had prepared in different locations."

"Cole, girl I got to go. No listen Tam, he hehehe! I had to drink whatever portion that was in the glass. When I finished, I was feeling some type of way. I know one thing, I wanted some dick! I wanted that mandingo so damn bad! He knew exactly what he had done! He would try to ignore me at times, but I would persist, and he couldn't help but give in to me. He had done the same thing before I entered the house. In fact, he was still drinking something when I came over."

"Cole girl, you know I want to hear all about it, but right now, I got to go honey!"

"Well, let me just tell you this! His thirteen-and-a-half-inch cock was super hard! That dick stood to full attention! It was trying to break out of the short he had on. He fucked me, and fucked me, and fucked me until I was almost unable to walk. We stopped for a moment, I mean a moment, and we were soon right back at it!"

"Girl Cole, I ain't mad at you! Go for it honey! I will get back with you soon."

After Kareem and I put it down for a couple of hours, I was worn the fuck out! I almost had lost all sense of reasoning. This man filled my every desire. He is truly to die for! It like wow! I can get really use to Dr. Feel Good Kareem. Now while he is asleep, I'm just going to call Lady Cole back so she would not suspect anything.

Ring, ring ring!

"Hey, Cole honey!"

"Oh hi Tam!"

"Girl I'm calling you back so I can get the rest of the 411 on Mr. Do Right Styles baby."

"Girl you so crazy Tam! He hehehe! Well, anyway, where was I? Oh yeah! After he had given me something to drink, I could tell he had been drinking pretty good before I came over. He had so much energy this time. I think Styles had taken some kind of enhancement or something because he was totally amped up and high energy. He was in beast mode Tam. He did tell me that he had tried some type of shit in the past and he wanted us to experience it together. I was like, hell nawl! But you know me, I gave in to him, and let me tell you! Honey! I was amped up right along with him! The shit was real! I don't know what it was. He asked me to trust him, so I did! Again, I don't know what the fuck it was, but I know home it made me feel."

"Honey, Mr. Styles has taken you to a whole 'nother dimension honey! I don't know what it was but that's why you got the hell fucked out of you! That hunk has turned the fire all the way up on your ass!"

"He pulled me all the way to the edge of the bed Tam. My ass dropped down off the mattress, he stood wide leg and firm as he gripped the floor and took his hands and placed them around my ankles and girl he began eating and licking my pussy while holding me in place. I was totally unable to move a muscle. I was under his complete control. He kinda commanded me to close my eyes and take three deep breaths. I did as he ask! In about five seconds, I felt totally invincible! He stood there for a moment and began slowly driving his huge dick in my wet pussy. I wanted more and more! I was unable to contain myself! I wanted more of Styles dick deep inside of me. I was uninhibited. I felt his shaft hitting my walls! That monster was driving me insane! It was the moment of truth. I could not return. I had now crossed a barrier that in previous times I would have never even thought about! I screamed countless times, not so much of it hurting! I screamed because like my boy Simone De says, 'It feel so good!'

"Girl, Tam, Listen to this! He fucked me for hours! Once again, we stopped and took a thirty-minute break. Honey, when I got up to look out of a window. This was in the guest bedroom. I saw one of those swings, you know those sex swings girl. I went back in the room where he was lying on the bed and asked him what in the hell is that in the room? He looked at me and began to smile! I said to him 'don't even try it Styles!' He continued to smile at me and said 'Don't worry, you're going to really like it! In fact, you're gonna really love it!' I looked at his ass and said 'Not me!' 'Auh, Cole!' I told his ass, 'Auh Cole my ass!' He turned on my boy Simone De jam, "Talk to Me Baby!" He held me and kissed me. I mean he was in charge. I had surrendered myself to him completely."

"Cole girl, how could handle all of that? It seems like you are having the time of your life! I say go for it chick! Hell, you only live once here! Go for the gusta!"

"Girl let me tell you this, I know you got to go! After this man had fucked me for what seemed like four hours. I was barely able to walk! His dick is so damn big, the head of it is wide like a mushroom! I feel every inch of it when he is penetrating me. Girl once he gets in his mood, it's over! His dick gets so damn hard; it sometime pulsates like a throbbing toothache. He loves for me to suck his dick. I must admit, Styles is a damn freak in every sense of the word. Girl, he likes for me to suck that big ass dick too! I can hardly put that big in my mouth. Tam girl, he has the nerves to choke somebody with the big ass anaconda dick. Girl he would give me specific instructions on how to suck that shit.

"He is so damn controlling! He would look at me as if you know what to do with this dick. He is no nonsense! Sometimes, he would just say, 'give me some head.' My mouth would be so damn tired. I mean he would actually shoot that shit right down my throat. The last time we were together, Tam, I was not myself at all. I really think Styles had given me something pretty strong because I can hardly remember every detail as to what transpired. I do know I was unable to walk when he finished fucking the hell out of me! I do remember entering the crib and he instructed me to drink from each glass throughout the house. I did as he instructed me. Shortly afterwards, I began to feel a lil funny. I remember my pussy was on fire! My hormones was raging, and all I wanted to do was fuck!

"I must say this time that Mr. Styles began kissing me as though there was no tomorrow. That shit really got my pussy over heated. He knew my trigger points at this time. This tall handsome black bulk walked through the house without a stitch of clothes on. I was getting hot as hell just watching that fuck stick dangling at first, and then before I knew it his shit was on super hard. He knew exactly what he was doing. I think for him, it was some kind of foreplay shit. When he turned to walk away from me, I would watch that perfectly shaped ass on him every time he walked. He was a sight for any woman. Although he was tall and well put together, he had slight bow legs and strong massive muscular thighs. This guy looks as though he was actually made, not born, but made!

"Tam, we nearly fucked in every room in house! I guess it was time to make it happen in the utility room. Check this shit out. Styles placed a towel on the washing machine. He open the lid, and stuck his hand inside and pulled the agitator to the side, which caused it to be off balance. I mean once he started the washing machine up it had a rough and rocky spin that was almost unimaginable. He called me over to him. I had no idea as to what his plan was. I hesitated for a moment. He gave me some kind of look as to say, 'get your ass over here now!' He jumped up and sat on top of the washing machine while the agitator was off balance and going around and around. I mean that shit was hitting the sides and bumping everything in its sight. Styles got this look on his face which said, 'You are about to ride this big black cock in a whole another vein.'

"He picked me up and sat me on that rock-hard thirteen-and-a-half-inch dick while the washer was knocking, humping, and bumping. I mean, this was total uncharted territory for me. Once again, that big, humongous dick was hard as any brick! The head of that shit has already stretched my shit like a bodybuilder stretching a rubber band. He sat me on that dick and instructed me to close my eyes and take three deep breaths. I did exactly as I was told! Shortly afterwards, I began to feel like I was on top of the world. I felt like I had no problems or worries. All I knew was, when I opened my eyes, he had given me so strong shit to inhale. I was like fuck! What in the hell was that! I felt totally, uninhibited. I felt myself wanting to fuck this find and negro without ceasing.

"Of course, Styles knew exactly what he was doing to me. I was green in the area of any kind of drug or sex enhancement. Girl Tam, once I got past the head of that monster, the head of that big as black dick began to fill my pussy up while bursting out the seams. He reached over and made some kind of adjustment to the washing cycle so that it could go to a rinse cycle. It was at this time that I knew without a shadow of a doubt, my ass was in trouble.

"That damn machine kicked, bumped, jumped, jerked—you name it. All I know is, his big thick cock was now buried in my pussy. I screamed like I had touched a hot coal. The faster the machine would spin, the more Styles would reach under my arm pits and grip my body while all the time holding me and being very careful not to let me go. He would look me in the face as I felt like I was going to pass the fuck out. He would say to me, while looking at me in the eyes, 'You getting fucked!' Take this damn dick! Ride this dick! I was gasping air. I felt like I was on the verge of fainting or something. I just know that I had lost all control of being able to say stop or wait or hold up. I could only agree with him as he looked me in the face and said, 'Yes you're getting fuck!'

"Tam, I'm telling you girl, I felt kinda stupid really, here I was involved with this man and I have lost all my faculties as for as being in control of the situation. It was clear to me at this point I had no control. It was also evident that the true nature of Styles was surfacing and his true color was shining through. He was into dominant sex. He likes to be in total control. He wouldn't take no or stop into consideration when he was in his zone of hardcore fucking."

"Cole girl, what are you going to do with this beast of a stallion?"

"I don't know Tam! That's just what I am saying, I can't do anything at this point. I'm afraid Tam, when Kareem gets home, my pussy will be worn the fuck out! I don't think I will have any walls, sides, or bottom to it. I'm really kinda freaked out about that! A man can tell if someone else has been hitting his girl. Shit, Tam, you know some times we will try and fake it. But a dick this fucking huge! Ain't no way to fake anything, I mean anything!

"We were on the floor fucking the other day. Styles reached over on the bed and grabbed some shit and told me to inhale it three times. I did what he ask. Girl Tam, the next thing I knew is this damn man had put two pillows under me while I was lying there on my back. He put his tennis shoes on and he grabbed both of my ankles, spread my legs as far apart as they could possible go. And he began to slow walk that monster dick inside my pussy. It felt good at first. Because you got to know my shit is sore as hell. But he stuck that dick in me and began long dicking me. He was hitting my spot. He has long found my G-spot. He takes advantage of knowing just what to do and how to do it. He would take his massive hands and kind of restrain me, as he position himself to fuck me like there will never be a tomorrow. He would drive the deep as deep in me as it could go. Then he would bring it out slowly until the tip the head was just touching my pussy.

"This shit was driving me fucking crazy! I was squirting cum everywhere. I felt like I was going to faint. The intensity of the climax was unlike anything I have ever experienced. I tried calling out his name, but I didn't have the strength. I was basically, much like damn zombie. After about thirty minutes of him long dicking me. He went fucking crazy on me. He literally started banging my pussy like he was gone fucking crazy. I screamed and screamed and screamed! 'Styles! Styles! Augh! Styles! My god! Wait! I can't!' 'Yes you can, take this dick! Take this motherfucking dick!' 'Oh Styles! I can't!'

"At that moment, he began licking me in my ears. Kissing me all over my neck and deep tonguing me. I was in no way to resist him at this point. I started screaming 'fuck me! Fuck me! Fuck me Styles! Please, I need your dick! I love your dick Styles! Please fuck me!' 'Come here suck this dick! Eat it!'"

"Girl, Cole, he do you like that!"

"Yes! This negro fucks the shit out of me! Tam, I tried to push him away, but he locked my hands in some kind of way, and went to town with me. Girl, Tam, he pulled the pillows from under me and pulled me towards him. He turned and straddled me in the sixty-nine position. He stuck that big behemoth in my mouth and started fucking the hell out of me in my mouth. He put the weight of his midsection to drive that dick down my throat. I began to choke on that shit. He was busy eating my pussy and fucking my mouth at the same time. This shit went on for about forty-five minutes.

"Before I knew anything I had locked my legs around his head because the dick was driving me the fuck crazy! Girl Tam, at that point, I didn't know whether to fuck, fight, or take flight. I just knew, I couldn't take too much more of this shit. But I must admit, the dick is damn good!

"Tam I'm gonna say this. I was already out of myself after drinking god knows what, and inhaling some kind of shit. I just felt a sense of euphoria. The next thing I realized was, I was forced to my knees with a hard thirteen-and-a-half-inch dick pressed against my lips. We were in the den area, He pressed my lips with that dick until I eventually opened my mouth. With a strong stern force, I felt the big anaconda sliding down my throat. When it hit my palate, that mother— kept going, driving that dick right on beyond my tonsils. I was unable to swallow or breathe. This shit was crazy. While this humongous dick was filling every inch of my mouth, I could feel each pulsation as it would swell more and more.

"I looked up at him and he was staring me right in my eyes. It was a look of dominance and control. I was going through all kinds of emotions. I felt his hands pressed around my neck as to slightly add a lil pressure for his sexual dominance and control. However, I reached up and placed my hands on his hands to show that I have some control or at least I would show some sense of trying. But he quickly rejected any notion of me rebuffing him. My head was bent slightly backwards as he pressed harder and harder trying to get more and more dick down my throat.

"Tears were rolling down my face. I could taste the salty pre-cum as it seeped out of this dick. I was in this position for quite a while, when all of a sudden I was lead over to a pallet on the floor. I observed ropes extending from four stationary positions. He looked at me with a strange look in his eyes and ask me if I was ready for the next chapter. I nodded my head with a faint yes, indicating that I was ready, at least I thought I was. He took control by pushing me down and tying my hands and legs to each rope. I was totally at his mercy.

"The next thing I knew, he was kissing me all over, whispering in my ears with that damn sexy-ass baritone voice and looking me deep in my eyes as to say, 'Let's do this.' I'm now thinking to myself, how could you allow this man to tie you up? Little did I know my world was about to take a turn at the hands of this man."

"Cole girl, what was he planning with you all tied up and shit?"

"Tam girl, Styles got on top of me, I was in for more than I ever bargain for. I felt his long wet tongue licking my stomach, navel, and thighs. Before I knew it, Styles was licking and sucking my pussy like it was candy. He buried his face deep in my pussy. I began feeding it to him with more intensity. I mean this man ate me like it was his last meal. I squirmed like a worm. Again, I realized I had no control. I began thinking to myself, 'God, what's going on? This man has taken me to a place I had never been before! I felt my body exploding over and over again!'

"Instead of trying to escape, I was now trying to feed him more and more. While still restrained, Styles turned his attention to sex. He got on top on me and I could feel his dick, that enormous cock penetrated me with no reserve. He went straight in my pussy with a sense of ownership. I believe at this time, Styles felt like he owned me. I believe he literally felt like I was his possession. I don't know what he was on or what he was using. Whatever it was, that shit worked! It was effective! He gave his a burst of energy, stamina, and potency like never before. The negro is a fucking sex machine!

"Styles fucked me in every position possible! While I was restrained, whatever position he could manage to flip me, turn me, twist me, stretch me, open me, trust me. He fucked me! At times, I would lie there and take the beating and not say a word. I had tapped the fuck out! I had resigned myself to feel it would be useless to say anything or do anything. I had no option, no control, I was at his mercy! At other time, I would scream to the of my lungs! The dick would hurt, it would feel good, it would drive me fucking out of my mind! Sometimes I would look at Styles while he would be fucking me, and sometimes, I would stare in silence. In other words, I would just lay there until he finished with me.

"Styles knew that, he had had his way with me for as long as I could stand it. I had experienced pain, pleasure, and passion until I reached intense climaxes. He later untied me, which allowed him to flex my body in many positions I had no idea I could accommodate. After untying me, this man walked me from room to room and continued to fuck me as if he had never had it before."

"Cole girl, you should—well, I don't know! Damn! I can't imagine! Cole! Girl, you have had quite an experience! That damn dick is good huh!"

"Yeah Tam! The dick is damn good! In fact, it's great! Honey the master blaster knows how to lay it down. He claim some shit as the 'art of the deal.'"

"What?"

"Yeah girl. He said he has mastered the art of fucking. All I can say to that is 'Amen!' That brother knows just how to please a woman one hundred percent!

"Before I was able to go home that day, Styles grabbed a chair in the bedroom. It was just a regular chair, the kind that would fit at a kitchen table. He put on Simone De's jam 'Bad Boy!' He sat down in the chair and began looking at me with his piercing brown eyes and ordered me to come over to him and sit in his lap. I said to Styles three or four times, that I needed to go. He kept saying it wouldn't take long. So I walked over to him and sat on him with my body facing him. Before I knew it, he was kissing me, licking me in my ears, and he just got carried away with my neck. He was licking and kissing! I was getting hotter and hotter. He reached over and got whatever the hell that was he was giving me whenever we were about to fuck. This time, he ordered me to take four deep breaths of it. That shit immediately took effect! I could remember being turned on like a water faucet on high. I began responding to every move he made. My body was on automatic pilot. He took his hand a gripped his dick and slowly maneuvered it in my pussy. He fucked me in the chair as hard as a boulder from Colorado. We were there in a rock hard chair with a rock hard dick in my pussy. I was unable to swarm in any direction trying to get away from Styles' massive cock.

"It was no use! I was under his spell, under his control, and under the influence of whatever that was he gave me. The dick was so deep inside of me I could hardly move. Styles kept ordering me to ride it. He would say it in a demanding voice. I was unable to tell if he was angry, or role-playing or what. I took one look at him and I felt like he was in another zone. I thought to myself, Styles was using so kind of enhancement for sex, and I didn't know what the side effects or what mindset he was in. What I do know is that, he sat at the edge of the chair, spread his legs, and gripped me under my arms and pulled me down deeper on that dick while sitting in that hard ass chair. I screamed to the top of my lungs! I cried out 'Styles! No! Styles! Please! No!' He took a look at me and said 'Shut the fuck up!' I said 'what?' He said 'you heard me. Shut the fuck up! Take this dick! Ride it! Grind on this dick!' I just let myself go, I gave up and in, and did what he directed me to do. I was being fucked mercilessly! I felt like this man is going to destroy my body. This big, black, handsome, sexy-ass, well-built man is tearing my pussy up. I screamed three times, and I heard Styles in his deep male voice holler as cum began to spew from his dick. I ain't gon lie, I enjoyed the fuck out of it!

"Okay Tam, girl, I'm gonna let you go. I know you're busy in Atlanta. I just had to call you and tell you what was going on girl!"

"I'm glad you did Cole! Girl, keep me posted."

"We'll have to have lunch when you're back in town."

"Okay, sure thing Cole!"

"Tam girl, I hope you get a chance to see Kareem while you're in Atlanta. You should try to have lunch with him. I really miss my boo! Kareem is such a great man! I will never trade him for anyone. He's my man, my friend, and most of all the father of my children. He's so silly at times. I can't wait till he's through with all this traveling so we can spend some quality time together."

"Okay Cole, maybe I will see him while I'm here. I'm not sure because I'm so busy. But hopefully we can have lunch."

"Hey baby!"

"Tam? Girl who is that? Sounds like you have company."

"Nawl, that was this guy standing close by."

Damn, hmmn, the voice sounds familiar.

"Okay Cole, we'll talk later."

Damn, wait a minute. Was that Kareem? I can't believe this shit! So wait a minute, it that what's been happening? Now all this shit is coming to light! Whenever Kareem goes out of town, Tam pretends she has a meeting or a product market for the boutique. I know goddamn well this bitch is not fucking Kareem! I will beat this bitch like she stole something! She don't know who the fuck I am! Let me find out this two-timing hoe is fucking Kareem. I'm gonna stomp that bitch in the ground! She don't know me! I took this bitch for my friend too! I welcomed that motherfucker in my home around my man and my children. I mean, I let her in on all of my business. Wow! All this shit is coming together now! What the fuck!

This motherfucking shit ain't going down like that! I overheard Kareem's voice, but they don't know it. Now watch the real Nicole! Watch the bitch Nicole rise up in me! Mr. Kareem, the good old doctor,

I guess he's been spending a lot of quality time doctoring on this bitch! But wait till I get hold to that ass! I'm gonna turn that motherfucker out! I got your number my bitch! Tam, whew, your ass is grass bitch, and I'm the lawn mower!

I'll call the hotel and book a rook right next to Dr. Kareem. They'll be surprised when they look up and see Mrs. Nicole!

***

A few days have passed and Dr. Kareem is already and prepared for his conference. He's calling me now.

"Hey bae!"

"Hi Kareem!"

"I miss you Cole!"

"I miss you to Kareem!"

"I can't wait to see you Cole. I got to make this going away stuff up to you."

"Auh, you so kind Kareem. I love you very much Dr. Kareem!"

"Okay the same here Cole. I'll be home soon! I will call you and let you know what day I'll be in."

"Okay baby, sounds great! Love you!"

"I love you too Cole!"

Now this negro thinks I'm a damn fool! He's in Atlanta getting him some new pussy from a bitch that's supposed to be my friend hoe! Oh wait, Kareem's calling back, maybe he sense something.

"Cole, are you okay?"

"Yeah baby, why you ask?"

"I just felt like you had something on your mind."

"No! I'm fine honey!"

"Okay we'll talk later."

"Sure thing baby, enjoy your conference honey! We only live once. Enjoy it to the fullest!"

"What? Cole!"

"Oh bae, I just want you to have a great time."

"Okay sweetheart, I will make sure I do just that! I will see you when I get back Cole."

"Okay honey!"

Now that motherfucker is dumb if he thinks I can't hear movement in the room other than him. I can hear someone right under him, but of course, I'm not supposed to know that he has anyone in the room with him, much less Tamera. Let me give that bitch a call, I bet she doesn't answer it. Ring, ring, ring, see I know what I'm talking about. I have called that bitch four times and have gotten no answer. I need my girl Ke to pop that motherfucking fan "BITCH" because this bitch is about to turn Atlanta, Georgia upside down!

Kareem knows I don't play! I'll put his ass on Bookface and social media and blow this shit up like an atomic bomb! I'm booking me a flight to Atlanta first thing in the morning! I'm about to tear that bitch up! Now that I think back on it, a woman's intuition is right ninety percent of the time. I felt somethin', but I never would have thought it would be this! I am pissed! It's because this hoe is supposed to be my friend, and now she's fucking my husband! Oh hell nawl! All the shit I have shared with her. I don't know, maybe she has told Kareem all about it. I don't know, and I don't give a flying fuck!

This is the Nicole I don't like to get all roused up and shit. I know exactly where Kareem is staying, and I made my reservation right next door to him. His ass and that bitch is about to get the worse surprise of their life.

Damn, there is Styles!

"Good morning Cole."

"Hello Styles."

"You're up mighty early."

"Yeah, I have to go out of town, something has come up, and I need to check on it."

"Damn baby, you sure everything is alright? Do you need me to go with you?"

"No Styles, thank you!"

"Wait baby, I could go with you, it's no problem. I could use my military benefit for an emergency situation. They will book me right away."

"Are you sure Styles?"

"Yes baby, I'm damn sure!"

"I could pay your way Styles."

"No, not at all, I can handle it! I just don't want you to be alone like this. I'm really concerned with you. You look damn pissed. But I got you! I'm with you baby!"

"Oh, thank you Styles! I think I'll only be there for a couple of days. While I take care of the business, you can rest in the hotel room."

"Rest, you think I need rest."

"Oh, I'm sure you're gonna need some rest! Ha hahaha!"

"Whatever Cole! Go get your shit."

"Styles!"

"Damn! It like that! I've seen a great change in you lately. I like it though. I like the feisty Nicole. In fact, that shit turns me on."

"Whatever Styles! You can ride to the airport with me. I'll leave my car and off to Atlanta we go."

"Would you like to tell me what's going on please?"

"Well, I think Kareem is fucking my best friend Tamera, so I'm about to show up unannounced."

"Damn! So are we going to war?"

"No, we are not going to war, but I am! Now Mr. Styles, don't get some kind of freaky shit in your head. We are strictly on business."

"Now come on Nicole, you know I wouldn't do anything like that baby. I'm a perfect gentleman."

"Whatever!"

Kareem and Tamera together in the hotel room.

"Hello sexy mama Tam Tam!"

"Hello sweet baby Kareem. I told you I would be here waiting for you. I intend to help you loosen up a bit. In fact, I plan on helping you wind all the way down tonight."

"Thank you Tam baby. I could use that. I am very tensed. I could use a good massage."

"Baby I'm about to get a shower Kareem. I will be out shortly."

"Okay baby, I will be waiting on you. Damn Tam! You look so damn sexy in that read negligee. You are one beautiful sexy ass woman. Damn girl, turn around and let me see how that thang fits you. Shit! It's perfect on you. Wow! Come here. Kiss me. Auh, yeah Tam, I want you baby."

"Auh, Kareem, that shit really turns me on. Oh, fuck! I can't take that shit. It makes me so weak when you stick your tongue in my ears. Oh my Kareem, Oh god! Baby, Kareem, I get so weak in my knees every time you kiss me on my neck."

"Here baby, take a sip of this. I made you a drink."

"Wow! What is that Kareem?"

"It's a lil something I mixed together. Here take another sip Tam."

"Damn, I'm already feeling like I'm paralyzed. That shit got me feeling damn good whatever it is."

"Come here Tam."

"Oh Kareem, I didn't know you could pick me up! He hehehe!"

"Yes baby, I can pick you up and I'm gonna put you in my bed."

"Auh! My god! Kareem!"

Scream!

"You're eating my pussy! Oh my god! Kareem, Kareem!"

Scream!

"Yeah you like that, don't you Tam."

"Eat that fucking pussy! Damn! Hell yeah! Kareem! I love it baby! Oh my god. You're sucking my nipples just right Kareem. I love it baby! Oh my, you're lying on top of me Kareem."

"Yeah I want you to spread your legs and wide as you can."

"Okay baby."

"Wider! That's right! That's how I want that pussy. Get ready for this big-ass dick."

"Auh! Kareem, it's so damn big baby! My god, you got it so deep in my pussy. Please wait Kareem."

"Give me your hands. I'll hold your hands while I fuck this pussy!"

"Oh yeah! Give it to me baby, give it to me Kareem! It's so damn good baby! Fuck me Kareem! Please give it to me baby! I love your dick! I love your long thick dick inside of me! Fuck me please! Oh my god! Fuck me Kareem please!"

"Give me your legs, hold them over your head Tam."

"Oh my! You got my legs all the way over my head! My toes are touching the pillow under my head."

"Kiss me Tam. Stick your tongue all the way down my throat."

"Oh Kareem! I'm going crazy when you lick my neck and stick your tongue in my ears. God you're fucking me crazy!"

Scream, scream, scream, scream!

"I'm cummin! I can't stop! Oh somebody help me, I can't take it no more!"

Scream! Scream, scream, scream!

"Goddamn! Give me that dick Kareem!"

"I'm about to cum Tam! Auh! Auh! Auh! My god! Damn whew! Shit! That pussy is the bomb. Oh my, I know it baby. I got you Tam. Here let's put my boy Simone De "Tonight Is the Night" on while I hold you sweetheart. Tam, girl you are a very sexy beautiful woman. I am a lucky man to be lying here with you tonight. I didn't know you were as beautiful inside as you are outside. Damn baby, I really enjoyed you tonight. Wait a minute, what happened to my massage Tam? Ha hahaha!"

"He hehehe! I don't know, I guess we got carried away."

"Well, to be quite honest baby, I'm glad we did."

One hour later, the both of us are sleeping. Kareem is drained and so am I. Plus the two of us have had a very busy week. Look at Dr. Kareem. He looks so handsome and peaceful lying there asleep. I guess I will get a few minutes in myself.

The moment after Tam and Kareem awake after a wild fucking.

"Hey baby."

"Hello Tam!"

"Looks like Tam put that thang on you and put you to sleep. He hehehe!"

"Yeah baby, it was good! I got to give it to you baby! It was damn good. That head you gave was fire too. I was thinking about it before I went to sleep. I even dreamed about that shit girl. In fact, I think it's a good time to get that massage."

"I hear you Dr. Kareem!"

"Yeah baby, I have a lot of tension in my neck and back. So the doctor is wondering if you could give him a little assistance. Auh baby, that was awesome."

"Dr. Kareem, your hands are simply amazing. I believe I can do the same thing. Come here Dr. Kareem, you know I'm gonna take good care of you."

"Thank you very much Tam, that's why I like you so much!"

"Wait a minute baby, let the good doctor take care of you! I know exactly that to look and feel for."

"Auh baby, that feels real good. Right there. Yeah, I love it baby. It really feels terrific."

"Here, let Dr. Kareem give you a thorough examination. I know exactly what to feel for. I know this body very well."

"Ah, yeah, right there Kareem. Oh yeah baby, that feels great."

"Wait a minute Tam, let's get totally comfortable. Here take all of this off. That's right. Let me work on this body naturally. Damn baby, you have one of the most gorgeous bodies I have ever seen."

"Thank you Kareem! That is so kind of you baby."

"How does this feel Tam?"

"Great Kareem. That feels great Kareem!"

"Here Tam turn over on your back. Let me work my magic on the front side of this masterpiece. I want you Tam. I need you Tam."

"Oh, Kareem, I'm all yours baby. I'm gonna love you like my boy Simone De said, "So Right So Good!"

"Oh Kareem, you really love Simone De's music don't you?"

"Hell yes! I mean, yeah baby. My boy in talented as hell. He sings soul music like that of the '70s and '80s, and he jams the shit out of them too. His music is for people with good taste in music. It's not for the club hoppers or people who just like a beat. His music is timeless and classy. Come here Tam, kiss me baby. I'm going to make sweet love to you. That's just what the good Doctor ordered. Come to me baby. Lay your head on daddy's chest."

"Oh Kareem, you feel so good."

"You feel even better Tam. I'm so happy to be here with you! I really love the way you make me feel."

"Oh Kareem, that feels great!"

"Yeah baby, daddy finna take good care of you baby."

"Damn Kareem, it looks like your man down there is growing by the seconds!"

"Ha hahaha! I not so sure if it has grown baby, but I damn sure know how to use it! Come here Tam, suck this dick! That's right baby, suck daddy's dick! I want you to make love to this dick. Anybody can suck a dick, but I want you to make love to this dick! Let it go down your throat. That's right! Now kiss it. Suck that head baby. Hummmn yeah! Fuck! Damn Tam! Baby you got that fire head. Shit! Open them legs Tam."

"Kareem—"

"Shuhhh! Open your legs!"

"Ouch! Damn Kareem! That dick is so damn huge! Auh! Damn! Fuck! Kareem you killing me! The dick is so damn big! I can't take it no more!"

"Yes you can baby. You can take it. I'm gonna fuck the hell out of you and make you take it. Who pussy is this?"

"Yours Kareem!"

"I can't hear you!"

"This your pussy Kareem!"

"If it's mine, fuck this dick like it's mine and don't fucking play with me!"

"Okay Kareem. Oh my god! Fuck me Kareem! I love it! I love your dick baby! I'm about to cum! I can't hold it!"

"No Tam! Wait! Don't cum yet!"

"I can't hold it Kareem. I can't!"

"I said wait, I will tell you when you can cum. Keep fucking this big dick! Get on top of it and ride this dick!"

"Oh Kareem! I don't know if I can. My god! It's so deep in me. Kareem!"

Scream, scream, scream!

"Auh! Auh! Damn! I'm cummin! Fuck me please! Give it to me baby! Fuck me!"

Scream, scream, scream!

"Your dick is still rock hard Kareem! I can't take it all. Look how much is left over. Damn long-ass anaconda!"

"Yeah, daddy is not through with you yet. I got you where I want you! Let me have the pussy! I got you! I got you! Turn the pussy a loose! Fuck this dick! Fuck this dick like it your last time! I got you baby! Let yourself go! I got you! Stop screaming Tam!"

Scream, scream, scream!

"I can't stop! Oh my god! You're killing my pussy Kareem!"

"This is what you wanted isn't it? Yes this is just what I been wanting for quite some time now. I been watching this ass. Now I got it, and I'm going to take damn good care of it!"

"Damn Kareem! You got my legs bent over my head, and you're standing up in my pussy. My god!"

Scream!

"I'm cummin!"

"I'm about to cum too Tam! Auh! Auh! Auh! Damn! Fuck! Auuh! Whew! That shit was crazy! Damn Tam! Are you okay? I hear you're breathing mighty hard over there."

"I'm sleepy Kareem."

"Go ahead baby and take a nap. I'm fucking tired my damn self! I was deep in that pussy. I stood all the way up in that shit. I sucked the fuck out of those nipples while I was fucking you! I pulled my dick in and out until the head hit the tip of those pussy lips. I tried to wear that pussy out! That shit was wet as hell! I got that shit open now! I own that hole! Hold on Tam, my phone is ringing. I bet it's Nicole! Nawl, whoever it was, hung up. I got to dictate my notes baby."

Damn, while Tam is sleeping, I got to make a few notes on this shit. Where is my recorder? Oh, here it is. Here I go: "Dr. Kareem, I fucked the shit out of Tam tonight in Atlanta, Georgia! I fucked this bitch like she was my fucking hoe or something! I stabbed that bitch with this big ass dick deep in that pussy! I fucked her as aggressive and rough as I have ever fucked anyone before. She screamed and hollered; however, I turned a deaf ear to her pleas, screams, and the fact that she tried her best to get away from this dick. I stood up in that pussy on my toes. I dug deep in the mattress and threw her legs over her head, and wore that hole out. I figured out her weak points on her body and used them to my advantage. I kissed her deeply, I kissed and lick her neck, I stuck my tongue in her ears, and she literally melted in my hands. At one point, I saw where she was gasping for air. I thought she was about to pass the fuck out! I pull her to the edge of the bed and man oh man. I dicked this bitch down in the worse way possible. After fucking her for a while in that position, I picked her up and placed her in the bed on her knees with them spread as far apart as she possibly could. Then mounted that pussy from behind. I stuck this dick in that wet pussy, she began to squirt pussy juice like a running faucet. I grabbed her head and tilted it back and I leaned over to her as began kissing her. I knew it would cause her to lose that ass to me totally. I kept saying to her, Tam, let the pussy go baby! Give me that pussy. I got you baby. I got you! Open that pussy baby! Arch that back! Open that pussy. She began to scream my name over, and over again. It was a great day. This bitch is built like a coke bottle. Damn! The damn word "fine" is an understatement!"

Let me turn my gadget off now. Unbelievable! I'm looking at that ass right now. She's lying there asleep, that ass is perfectly shaped. I beat those walls down. I kept teasing that pussy by driving this dick in and out of that hole. At one point my dick came out of that hole, that shit was so wet. However, she reached down and grabbed that dick, and put it back in there quickly! That bitch couldn't stop cummin! She was going insane! I fucked her until I thought she had enough. I think my dick was growing and growing bigger and bigger.

What she don't know is I had swallowed two Viagras. That shit got me wired right off the bat! I'm ready to go again. I'm gonna let her get a lil sleep, but I'm gonna tear that ass up again. She needs her rest right now. When she stood up after I wrecked that pussy, her body went limp. I hurried over to catch her in a flash. But she don't know, I gonna beat that ass up good tonight!

Shortly afterwards, Tam got out of bed and barely made her way to the restroom where she mustered up strength to take a shower. I sat in the bedroom drinking a glass of wine and listening to a lil music. In about fifteen minutes, Tam made her way out of the shower and entered the bedroom. We sat on the bed holding each other while the both of us was basically almost in a trance at what had transpired between the two of us.

We eventually moved to the sitting room in the hotel and talked for maybe twenty minutes. I got up to change out the cd and put Simone De's jam in "Come and go with me!" While the music was playing, we could hear someone outside the door chatting or talking at a low voice. We could clearly hear something, but we were unable to make out who or what they were saying. We could hear keys and shatter, but we wrote it off to be hotel guest checking in.

We could hear when they got the door open and eventually they went inside the room. Within an hour, we could smell the aroma of gourmet food coming from the next room over. Then there was soft music playing as if someone had planned a very romantic evening.

I thought to myself, that's what I'm talking about. A man and his lady enjoying a quiet romantic night. Wait a minute, It didn't take a long for them to get at it. I mean, they are really going at it! Shit, whatever bruh is doing, he is damn sure laying it down. I mean she is screaming to the top of her lungs.

"Damn wake up Tam. Babe, this dude is killing his girl over there. Listen to that shit. I sounds like he has some kind of muffle over her mouth. I can hear him telling her to suck that dick. Oh shit! She's riding that nigga now. Stand right here Tam."

"Oh my god! He is beating her down. Oh my goodness. I could never take anything like that."

"Here Tam, put your ear right here."

"Okay, we should be ashamed Kareem."

"I know baby, but it's kinda interesting. I mean bruh is in that shit! Listen Tam, he's telling her to lay on her back. Damn! Listen to that shit! She keep saying it's too damn big, but bruh keep driving that shit looks like. I keep hearing her say, oh my god. Damn, I'm still kind of tipsy myself. But this shit is like watching, well better yet, listening to porn. I know some damn body is going to call the front desk and report their ass. Hey Tam, I'm about to go down and have a few drinks at the bar. Would you like to accompany me?"

"No baby, I'm going to get a shower and relax a little."

"Okay sweetheart. I'll be back soon Tam."

I'll take the stairs and get a lil exercise it'll do me good. Here I am, finally reached the first floor. Damn, this shit is exquisite! I really like this set-up. The music is nice and romantic. Damn that is an extravagant set-up in here along with a beautiful water fountain. The light in here are calming and romantic. Damn, I should have brought Tam down with me. Hey, what do you know! They're playing my Simone De's "Wanna Be Your Lover." This shit is right!

I think I'll order drink. There aren't that many people in here today night. There's a brother over there. Looks like he's pretty cool. I'm gonna walk over and introduce myself to him.

"What's up my brother? You got it man. I'm Kareem."

"What's up brother? I'm Styles."

"Please to meet you man. Why don't you join me Styles?"

"Thank you man! I really appreciate that Kareem. This is a nice set-up here man."

"Hell yeah! They laid it out Styles. It's really tasteful. Are you from here Styles?"

"Nawl man, I flew in a few hours ago. Just here in the city with a lady friend of mine."

"Okay cool!"

"Yeah man, she has to handle some business. So, she ask me if I would fly out here with her. So hell, I wasn't doing anything so I took her up on her offer."

"I got you bruh! I been here for a few days myself with my job, so really, I been hanging out here for a minute."

"Shit, I see some few sharp, sexy ass ladies on the other side of the room."

"Shit bruh, I have already checked them out, but I got an old girl upstairs, she pretty tight."

"I got you my brother."

"I'm about to go back up to my room Kareem. Perhaps if we're here on Friday, maybe we can get together and workout a lil bit."

"Cool man, I'm good with that."

"Alright then, that sounds like a plan. Okay, nice meeting you Styles."

"You too Kareem. Later my brother. Bet!"

***

"Hey baby, how was it at the bar?"

"It was cool Nicole. I met a cool dude down there. We're supposed to work out a little Friday."

"Really, that was quick!"

"Well, it was, but me and ole dude hit it off really good. What have you been up to since I been gone?"

"Not too much, I got a shower and fixed a drink, that's about it!"

***

"Hi Kareem!"

"Hello baby."

"You wasn't there too long."

"No I wasn't. I just wanted to get a drink and just relax a little. I love the set-up in the bar area and I just wanted to take advantage of the scenery. I think this area only caters to high rollers. You could tell the creme de la creme only come here and hang out."

"I agree Kareem. You are probably right about that! What can Tam Tam do for you?"

"Well now, as a matter of fact, you know baby every time I get around you, my dick gets hard as a fucking brick!"

"Well baby, that's just fine! I know exactly what to do with it."

"Yeah! I know you do. You have already proven that bae. How about giving daddy a taste of what you have in store for me."

"Sure! Anything for my Kareem."

"Alright then my sweet thang. Come on over here. Bring me that hot sexy pussy."

"You're so crazy Kareem, let me show you some real shit. I'm going to take good care of that big ole ass anaconda. I ain't gone lie about it, the big ass monster was damn good. You stood up in my pussy thinking you were Theodis doing some stand up in it type of shit. Come here Kareem, lay down baby."

"Auh, yeah, let daddy lay on my back while mama take good care of me."

"You are a sexy-ass man Kareem."

"Thank you baby. You are even more sexy Tamera."

"Here, take off these clothes Kareem. Here I will help you."

"Okay great. I will help you as well Tam."

"Oh, Kareem! Your dick is huge baby! I know I've said it before! But this shit is humongous!"

"It's just more to love you with Tam."

"I mean it never cease to amaze me how big it is. I love everything about you! Kiss me Kareem."

"Come here Tamera hmmn. I love the way you sink your tongue down my throat. I feel the warmth of your body."

"Lay all the way back Kareem."

"Damn Tam, that shit feels good baby. Keep it right there. Yeah suck it hard for me. Yeah that's right, that's right. Kiss that head for me baby. Look up at me when you're sucking that dick. Stick it back in your mouth. Suck that dick! Keep it wet for me. Yeah, just like that. Don't stop! Yeah, go all the way down on that dick. Choke on that dick baby. Suck it! Don't stop baby! Suck that dick good! Damn! Come here let me taste that pussy."

"Auh! Oh Kareem! Oh my god! Hmmnn! Oh yeah, Kareem, baby, shit! Oh my god! It feels so damn good Kareem. I love it baby. Oh my, I'm about to cum! Kareem!"

Scream, scream, scream!

"Come here let me fuck this pussy!"

"Oh Kareem!"

"Oh Kareem my ass, I'm finna fuck this pussy. Auh! Auh!"

"My god! Wait!"

"Relax baby, it's in there now. Take the dick. Yeah, yeah! Relax baby, give daddy the pussy. Let me fuck you good. Let the pussy go! I got you! I got you baby!"

"Yeah, oh Kareem, oh my god! Oh fuck me Kareem! I love your dick! Please baby, don't stop! Keep it right there! Keep it right there! Oh my, I'm cummin! Kareem please fuck me!"

"I'm about to bust too baby! Auuuuh! Damn Tam! Auuuuh! Fuck!"

Scream!

"Kareem! I'm cummin! Oh my god!"

"Shit Tam! Whew! That shit was crazy! Damn I got to relax a minute. You like to get fucked rough don't you Tam!"

"Be quiet."

"Come on and admit to it baby. I already know. I just want to hear you say it."

"I like to be handled by a real man Kareem. Yes! If you must know."

One hour later.

"Kareem, what are you doing?"

"I want to make love to my girl. Come here Tam. I find it very difficult to resist you. You turns me on Tam like a water faucet."

"Kareem, that goes without saying baby. I get weak in the knees whenever we're together. You make me feel so damn good. Oh baby, I love it when you suck and kiss on my neck. I love when you stick your tongue in my ear. You know that is my weak spot. I lose all sense of control baby. I literally begin to melt. Oh baby, Kareem you're sucking my nipples. Aren't you a little tired baby?"

"No baby, not at all. Auh, that feels so good. Keep kissing my tits like that, you're gonna start something."

"How does it feel Tam?"

"I love it Kareem!"

"Tam baby, let's just take advantage of this moment. I know we been going at it, but I got something different I want to do to you. Something different!"

"What do you mean Kareem? You have done everything possible to me already."

"Really baby, I haven't! I have a dark side to me when it comes to having sex. For the most part, at home, I handle my business. But for real, I like to be kinky and rough, and I don't feel like Nicole is really into it. Plus, I don't think I could really let myself go and have my way with her like I really want to."

"Oh, so you want to the things to me that you don't feel like you can't do to your wife."

"No baby, don't take it like that! I just feel very comfortable with you, and I don't want to hold back on you at all. I love making love to you. Well, really, if the true me is allowed to come out, I would like to say it in another way."

"Mr. Kareem, what would that other way be?"

"I would like to just look at you and stare for a moment, with a very demanding and dominant look, and say, 'I want to fuck you again!'"

"Oh Kareem, baby by all mean please be yourself!"

"Thank you baby! I promise not to tear that pussy up too bad!"

"Whatever!"

"Please, well this time is gonna be a killa girl. I'm gonna use some language and control mechanism that won't wait! You in?"

"Yeah, I guess I'm in! But no tying me up! That shit ain't gone fly."

"I got you baby! Okay, I got something for us to try."

"What's that?"

"Remember now, you do as I tell you to do. Here Tam, I want you to try this drink. I fixed it for you myself. Drink it all!"

"Oh Kareem . . ."

"Drink it baby. I want you to feel good when I beat that pussy down this time. Come on in the sitting room Tam. I took one of the damn blue pills and that shit is working! My damn dick is rock hard! Look at that shit! Put your hands around it and massage it for me. Damn baby, that feels good. Go down on your knees and suck daddy's dick real good. Look up at me while you suck my dick. Yeah, that's' right suck it."

"Oh Kareem. I can't breathe, you're choking me, I can't breathe."

"You just suck this dick! You don't need breath to suck dick. Just suck it! Just suck it!"

"I need to catch my breath Kareem! My God you had it all the down my throat."

"Lay on your back."

"Kareem please!"

"Just do as I say and lay back on your back. I'm gonna fuck that mouth! Oh! Ooooo, oooo, hmmmn. Come on bitch! Suck it Tam! Take all of it! I want you to take every inch of this pipe. I gonna fuck you like you have never had it before! Open your legs!"

"Kareem, please wait! I'm sore! My pussy is throbbing. It's feel like it is twice its size. I don't think I can take it anymore! My god!"

"Open your legs bitch and take this dick! You can do it the easy way, or you can do it the hard way. But rest assured, you're going to do it."

"Okay Kareem, I want it, but I'm not sure I can take anymore. Open it up!"

"Auuuh! Auuuh! Oh my! Damn it's too big! Auuuh! Kareem! Oh my god! I can't!"

"Yes you can! I got you baby, just take the dick!"

"It's too big Kareem! It hurts!"

"Shut the fuck up and take the dick! Kiss me. That's right stick your tongue down my throat. Just let yourself go. I got you!"

"Oh Kareem, please, you got your tongue in my ears. You know that drives me crazy! Fuck me Kareem! I'm feeling so good right now baby! I don't know what was in the drink, but I can feel it kicking in on me now! Come on Kareem, fuck me baby! Oh! You so deep in me Kareem. I feel you deep in my guts! Take me! Fuck me! I don't fucking care anymore! This is your pussy Kareem! This is your pussy daddy! Give it all to me. I need you Kareem."

"You gonna be my bitch?"

"Yes! I will be your bitch."

"You gonna do what I tell you to do?"

"Yes! I will do whatever you tell me to do. Oh yeah Kareem, keep it right there! Fuck me right there! I cummin Kareem! I cummig! Fuck me! Fuck me! Fuck me! Oh my god! Oh my god! Please don't stop!"

"Open that pussy bitch! Auuuh! I'm about to cum Tam! Oh! Hell yeah! Oh shit! Damn! Ohhhh! Ohhhh! Shit! Damn, that shit was crazy! I was so deep in you I could feel your guts. Damn girl, I hope no one heard you with all that hollering and shit."

"Damn, what's that noise? I hear something pounding and knocking, shit that sounds like somebody else is going at it vigorously! Dammn! That homie is beating that shit. I mean he is beating her back in! The damn bed post is hitting the walls and shit. Whomever that chick is over there is getting that pussy stomped! I mean that dude is banging the hell out of her! Damn Tam! I wonder if anybody heard us when we were going at it?"

"I sure as hell hope not!"

"That bitch is screaming like dude is boning thirteen and a half inches in her!"

"Damn Kareem, you damn sure ain't lying. It sounds like he has muffled her mouth with a pillow or something. I feel for the old girl."

"Homeboy ain't playing! Shit, that's been going on down for an hour. Come here Tam. Were going to turn up too!"

"No baby! I can't take it no more!"

"Yes you can. Come here. Get on top of me and ride this dick! Wait a minute, I got a little something that might help you."

"What is it?"

"Just hold on a minute. I'll get it out of my bag. Close your eyes Tam."

"What is it Kareem?"

"Close your eyes and do as I say! Here you go, take it. I want you to take a deep breath Tam. That's right take another one for daddy. Take one more baby."

"Kareem no! Whew! Kareem, I feel so good baby! I'm so mellow I want you to fuck me Kareem! I feel so damn hot and sexy! I want you to fuck me good. You own this pussy Kareem! It's yours!"

"That's what I want to hear. Get on your knees Tam spread your legs wide and arch that back. I'm gonna beat that pussy from behind."

"Auuh! Kareem, give it to me!"

"I got you Tam!"

"Give it to me Kareem!"

"Keep that back arch!"

"Oh my! Kareem, you spanked my ass too hard!"

Spank!

"Oh Kareem! That hurts!"

Spank!

"Oh Kareem, you are turning me out. Give me that dick baby!"

"I knew you would like it. In fact, you're gonna love it! Keep those legs spread and that ass arched. Now take all of this dick. I'm about to hit that shit twenty times. No! shut the fuck up! Let me wrap this belt around your waist first. Now I got something that will hold you in place. Bang! Oh! Count it bitch!"

"Kareem you're killing me!"

"Keep counting or I'm starting all over."

"Kareem, I'm about to pass out! I'm cummin! Deeper Kareem! I'm cummin! I can't stop!"

"Let it go Tam! I got you baby! Get on top of this dick and ride until I tell you to stop! Ride it! Go, twenty times without stopping. Then grind it twenty times. Then get on your knees and face me with that dick still in that pussy. You better not let it come out! Fuck me Tam! Yeah, that's my bitch. That's my bitch. Fuck me Tam. Love the dick. Put it in your mouth. Eat dick! Eat dick! Eat dick! Shit, Tam I'm cummin! Take all of it! Eat dick! I want to give you what you really been longing for Tam. I am pretty good with gauging women. I can tell most of the time what they want or what they don't want. I can basically read your energy and tap into you psychic and gauge what a woman is feeling."

"Oh Kareem, you think you are so smart he hehehe! No baby, I just have this thing, you can call it male intuition, sixth sense, whatever. I usually get it right each time. Let's face it, I was able to tap into your psychic and discover all the naughty things you wanted me to do to you."

"Oh stop Kareem! Ha hahaha!"

"Now what do you have to say about that Ms. Tamera?"

"I have absolutely nothing to say Dr. Kareem."

"Well, answer my question Ms. Tam. Was I right about you or was I wrong?"

"I think you know the answer to that Dr. Kareem or Dr. Phil or whatever!"

"Ha hahaha! Don't get all bent out of shape Ms. Tamera, I'm just trying to prove a point. Hey baby, listen. They're going at it again in the room next door. Oh dude whoever he is, is beating that shit down again. Damn! You hear that Tam! He's beating that shit! I hear her saying put me down, it's too big!"

"You ain't never lied Kareem. Whoever he is, he is in that shit."

"Let's get to the wall and be noisy. Ha hahaha! Come on Tam, really that shit is turning me on like fuck! He told her to get to the edge of the bed. Oh shit! He's folding her over. I hear her saying you got my legs bent over my head. Yeah baby, drop that ass off the edge of the bed a lil for me. Listen Tam. He killing her! What the fuck is she saying? Thirteen and a half inches! Is she saying what I think she said?"

"Yes Kareem, she's telling him he's got all thirteen and a half inches in her. She screaming like crazy! He's telling her this is how I like to fuck you. I wanted to stand here at the edge of the bed and spread your legs wide open and drop that ass off the bed and dick you down till times get better. I'm gonna fuck this pussy tonight!"

***

"Oh please! I can't take it no more!"

"Come here and kiss me. You wanted to rough fuck right! You told me to call you names while I fuck you. This what you want? Is it bitch! Give me that pussy! Kiss me! Take this damn dick bitch! Wet this dick up! I ain't gone let up until you cum in this position. I got this pussy now, and it ain't shit you can do about it! Give it to me! Give it to me! Give it to me! Open that pussy up bitch! This how you want me to treat you? You gonna always be my bitch! Even when your husband gets home. I'm still gonna fuck this pussy. I ought to put my name on it. Who pussy is this?"

"Oh my god!"

"I said who pussy is this?"

"Auuuh! Please, I can't take it no more!"

"Oh, so you not gonna answer me huh! Okay! Get to the edge of the bed. Stand facing the bed. Now spread them legs."

"Auh! My god, I can't!"

***

"Tam, whoever he is in the room next door, I know one damn thing, he's not leaving that pussy to chance. He's taking that shit out! I mean my boy is beating the damn bass drum with a damn telegram pole. Wow! She's screaming for mercy!"

"What's so damn funny Dr. Kareem?"

"Nothing baby, I'm just glad the brother is releasing some much built-up pressure."

***

"Lay on the floor."

"No! Please baby, I can't take it! Oh put me down."

"Get on the damn floor, now spread them legs. I'm finna fuck you something crazy!"

"Oh it so big babe."

"That pussy is red! That shit is on fire! Kiss me."

"Oh my! Fuck me please I can't control myself any more. Please fuck me good! I need it! Please fuck me with that huge dick! Give it all to me please! Fuck me sir! Fuck me! This is your pussy!"

"You damn right, this is my pussy, and don't you forget it!

***

"Tam you know, I want to fuck right?"

"No baby, let's wait a while."

"Wait! Wait for what? I want to fuck! I want that ass now baby."

"Hold up Kareem, give me a minute baby."

"Just a little bit Tam. Hey listen, front desk is calling them, apparently someone called and reported them fucking like crazy. Ha hahaha!"

"That shit is not funny Kareem."

"Why are you so uptight? She's getting what she wanted, and old dude just handling his business. You know what Tam, it sure does seem like I hear a familiar voice in that room. I know that shit is crazy, but it damn sure seem like it. Damn, they're calling that room again! Ha hahaha! That shit is funny! I'm surprised they didn't call our room when I was beating your back out."

"Maybe we just didn't hear it."

"Yeah right, you were fucked up after drinking that shit. You don't know if they called or not!"

"By the way they did call, at least someone did, but you were too busy trying to fuck another hole in me."

"I love fucking that pussy bae. I love making love to you."

"Making love to me! Where did you get that shit from? How about when you were fucking the hell out of me!"

"Damn they must have had one too many! I'm telling you it seems like I hear a familiar voice coming from that room. Damn! I must be losing it! Come on Tam, l et's get a shower."

"Okay Kareem."

"They will be serving dinner in an hour."

"Okay Kareem, however, I am not so sure I can make it."

"What do you mean?"

"I mean you have fucked me senseless!"

"Come on baby, let's get a shower and get dressed. We'll go down and check things out."

***

"Nicole baby, are you okay?"

"Styles, You can't continue to fuck me like this. I won't be any good to anyone! Especially to Kareem when he wants to have sex. I am totally exhausted!

"Auh, come on Nicole, you know you like it like that! Stop pretending. You like when I take control and fuck that pussy the way I want to."

"Styles! Stop it."

"Okay Cole, the next time, I won't beat it down so bad. I'll take good care of you! Come baby, let's get a shower and go down for dinner."

"Sure baby, that sounds great!"

"Wow! You are simply stunning baby! Nicole you are a beauty queen. Honey you are one sexy black goddess! It didn't take anytime for you to transform."

"What?"

"You know what I mean baby. Ha hahaha!"

"Ha hahaha hell!"

"Come on Cole, have a sense of humor."

"Whatever Styles! Now look at you Mr. Styles! You are the most sexiest, handsome, debonair man I have seen in quite some time, and that's only because I haven't seen Kareem in a minute. He hehehe!"

"He hehehe my ass!"

"Stop Styles! You know I'm just kidding with you sir! You are really one of the most well put together men I have ever seen. I don't have a problem telling you that! When I first laid eyes on you, you were breathtaking. Even this very moment, you are still breathtaking. You are really quite a guy Mr. Styles!"

"Tell me this Ms. Nicole, am I your guy? Look at me in my eyes and answer me."

"Yes, you are certainly my guy Styles! I am digging you more than you'll ever know!"

"Well Ms. Nicole. It's up to you to make me know how you feel. Come here girl and give your daddy a kiss."

"He hehehe!"

"What's the laughter for Cole?"

"Nothing really, I'm just laughing. Can't a girl laugh?"

"Come on Cole, let's go down for dinner."

Oh, the Shit Hits the Fan! The Four Meet Up.

"Kareem, let's sit over here."

"Okay Tamera, this is a very nice spot. Actually the place is a little crowded. This area sits four and it's only two of us."

"I know baby. I just like this view. The place is so magnificent."

"Hey, there goes the dude I met earlier. I'll ask him to come over and sit with us if you don't mind."

"No, I really don't mind."

"Hey what's up brother?"

"What's up my man?"

"Why don't you all sit here with us."

"Well I appreciate it, but my girl had to make a call. Her daughter just called her a few minutes ago."

"Please, there's plenty of room!"

"Are you sure?"

"Yes, I'm very sure! In fact, I insist brother! Sit here, and your girl can join us when she returns."

"Once again man, I really appreciate you guys! Let me check on her. She should be back by now. Excuse me, I'll be right back."

Goddamn! Fireworks! Tamera, Nicole, Styles, and Kareem Meet!

"Hello everyone! This is Nicole!"

"What the fuck is this? Hello this is Nicole! This bitch knows who I am! You could have seen the expression on Kareem's face."

"Hello Cole!"

"Don't hello Cole me Kareem! What the fuck is this! Why are you having dinner with this bitch?"

"Wait one damn minute Nicole! Now, you can address me better than that!"

"Bitch I don't have to address you better than a damn thang! You answer my question! I want to know why are you here with my motherfucking husband bitch?"

"Cole, wait baby! I can explain baby!"

"You got five seconds to do so, or I'm turning this motherfucker out!"

"Hold on Nicole!"

"You shut the fuck up too Styles!"

"Hey wait a minute, you don't talk to me like that!"

"Shut the fuck up Styles!"

"You the guy I met earlier. You told me you had a chick here who you're traveling with, and you were handling your business! Motherfucker, this is my damn wife you fucking! What the fuck is going on with that Nicole!"

"Hold on brother!"

"Man, fuck you, don't talk that shit to me! Brother my damn ass! Your puck ass, hoe ass dog!"

"Well, I beg to differ, and your wife could vouch that I'm not puck."

"Man I'll tear in your ass! I don't suggest it. In fact, back the fuck up."

"This shit is crazy!"

"Tam shut the fuck up because you haven't seen crazy yet hoe!"

Kareem reflects.

"Wait a minute, what the fuck is going on here! Nicole what room number are you staying in?"

"Why?"

"I ask you a question Nicole!"

"I'm in suite 346, what else you need to know?"

"Oh! So that's the wild fucking noise we've been listening to! So now, that's the room the front desk had to call because of the wild erotic loud fucking!"

"Well, well, Ms. Nicole!"

"Bitch don't you say a damn thang to me!"

"Well, she's damn sure telling the truth Nicole!"

"How long you been fucking this man?"

"Oh please Kareem, don't try and flip the script on me! This bitch is supposed to be my friend and she's fucking my man!"

"Well bitch, to be honest, you fucking somebody else man. So what is the fucking difference!"

"The difference hoe is, you are supposed to be my motherfucking friend bitch, but you too busy being a fucking homewrecker."

"Kareem, what the fuck do you have to say about all of this? You're supposed to be attending a conference, I bet you are! You better give me some damn answers, and give them now, or about to turn this bitch out!"

"Ma'am, I'm with the management team. I need you all to calm down as we are having complaints from other customers."

"Let's take this shit outside before I clown in this bitch! Tam, I want to see your ass outside bitch, I'm not through with you!"

"Bitch, I will oblige you because I'm not through with your ass either!"

"Tam, what in the hell is wrong with you? I don't believe this shit! You are supposed to be my BFF, but that shit is out the window! How could you betray me like that? After all we have been through together, and all I have shared with you, and this is the thanks I get from you."

"Wait a minute Nicole! Let me tell you one damn thang! You want to have your cake and ice cream, and that's fine! You want both men! Each day you shared your information about how good Kareem what tearing up your pussy, bitch mine was getting wet just listening to you with that shit! You put me right in the middle of your business. I was minding my own damn business. So bitch you brought me on it! There were times when you would share your business with me, I could hardly contain myself! I would get so damn hot until my pussy would literally blow steam. My hormones was running wild and my drawers soaking wet. But I endured that shit trying to support you."

"Wait a minute Tam!"

"No bitch you wait a minute! I don't appreciate you coming in the dinner hall acting like you're Lily White or Miss goody-two-shoes!"

"How long have you been sleeping with Kareem?"

"We don't need to go there Nicole."

"Tam, I ask you a damn question, and I want a goddamn answer!"

"Well, if you must know, Kareem and I have been sleeping together for five months."

"What!"

"Yes five months, and I have to tell you the dick is damn good, huh, just as good as Mr. Styles!"

"Wait a minute bitch!"

"I'm not waiting a goddamn thang!"

"Bitch, you're not gonna disrespect me Tam!"

"Honey gone on, the respect flew out the window when you started sucking Styles dick! Don't forget, I can write a fucking book on you two!"

"You can't do a motherfucking thang!"

"Bitch, just watch me!"

"What I want to do right now Ms. Tam is beat your damn ass!"

"Hold on hoe! Now, you may hit me, but, don't be so sure you're gonna beat my ass. In order to beat some ass, you got to bring some ass!"

"I want you to know, Mrs. Tam, I'll roll with your goddamn ass."

"Bitch don't you go there with me! So you been fucking Kareem for five months! Okay, trick, you wanna play that shit! Bam!"

"Oh! Bitch you slapped me!"

"I sure did!"

"Bitch don't nobody slap Tamera and get away with it! Whap! Bam!"

"Hey Nicole and Tam, y'all stop that fighting out here! Hey come on ladies!"

"You shut the fuck up Kareem! I'm about to beat this bitch ass."

"Come on Nicole!"

"I felt like some shit was going on, that's why I flew here!"

"Come on Cole!"

"Don't come on Cole me Dr. Motherfucking Feel Good! You gonna get yours too!"

"Come on Cole!"

"Wait Styles!"

"Hey man don't say shit to my wife Mr. Styles!"

"Hey brother, this ain't what you want!"

"Hey man don't get your fucking drawers in a wad! Don't disrespect me my brother Styles!"

"What the fuck you mean man, the good doctor. You been out here fucking someone else while you claim to be attending medical conferences and shit!"

"How in the fuck do you know? By the way, where in the fuck did you come from? How in the hell did you meet my wife? Boy, you got some explaining to do!"

"Hey man, don't underestimate me my brother. This ain't what you want."

"Don't think your girl has been home doing without! Oh, she has had her share of dick in the last few weeks. I mean she has had her share of dick like the fucking world was coming to an end. I'm surprised she is able to walk or talk for that matter! I know what the fuck I'm talking about too!"

"Tam, you fuckin bitch! You can run your mouth, and I will close it for you!"

"Oh, now you're threatening me!"

"No, don't look at it as a threat! Just look at it as being the goddamn truth!"

"Oh, so, Nicole, you been fucking this negro while I was away?"

"Kareem!"

"Baby, don't Kareem me right about now. I ask you a question! Have you been fucking Mr. Styles, or whatever while I was away?"

"Kareem! Brother let me help you out."

"Hey man don't 'brother' me!"

"I just want you to know Dr. Kareem, actually, we fucked several times while you were in town. I just want you to know man to man."

"Man shut the fuck up! You got one more word to say to me! I will destroy your black ass!"

"Well, good doctor, do what you think you must. I just wanted you to know I been dicking your girl like there's no tomorrow! The best part about it, she enjoyed every moment of it. I mean I'm not trying to front, or stunt, but I'm packing thirteen and a half inches, and each time, I made damn sure she got every inch of it. Oh, by the way, Cole like the dick best while laying on her back with her legs throwed over her head. I would just position the dick in that hot, wet pussy and fuck the hell out of her. I would stand up in it until she cum and scream my name over and over again. Ha hahaha! Dr. Kareem, that's the art of the deal!"

"Nicole, I need to see you now! Is that true?"

"Yes Kareem. It's true. I'm very sorry!"

"Yeah, I bet you are! I just bet the fuck you are! I guess you're sorry you got caught, but not sorry for fucking another man. Damn! That shit is whack! I don't believe this shit! So, you been fucking this sorry piece of shit!"

"Kareem, I just got caught up in something I didn't quite know how to get out of. I am sorry."

"I'm not believing this shit, I mean, I got out of town trying to make things nice and provide you with the kind of lifestyles you choose to live and this the thanks I get."

"No Kareem. That's not the truth. But wait a minute here, don't stand here as if you are Mr. Do Right. What do you have to say for yourself? You have this bitch out here when I'm thinking you are away attending a medical conference! I guess Ms. Tam is the main attraction huh! That bitch is supposed to be my friend, and she is here laying up in the hotel room with my man with her damn legs spread wide open. How do you explain that shit?"

"Baby, really, I can't! I'm sorry! I was wrong."

"I will deal with your ass when we get home! Her ass is mine!"

"Wait a minute baby, I don't think you are all that innocent! Tam filled me in on you and Mr. Styles. I can't believe all the shit she told me that you two have been doing. I cannot believe you would go along with all the shit she shared with me. I was told that you are damn near his sex slave."

"Oh please Kareem!"

"Nawl, I want to know if that shit is true! It's not like you two were having a one-night stand. This shit has been going on for some time! So don't stand here and act like you are all good and shit!"

"Hey bruh, you and I can talk."

"Shut the fuck up Styles!"

"That's right man, you don't have a fucking thang to say to me! You violated bruh! You know Nicole was married, but you played on her vulnerable state. You ain't no damn good my boy!"

"Kareem!"

"Boy! Who in the hell are you calling a boy! I got your damn boy! I told you, your wife can vouch that I'm all man."

"Kareem calm down please."

"Nawl baby, I'm gone tell this damn clown about himself! You are a sorry piece of shit!"

"Hey brother, since you want to go out like that, yeah I fucked your wife! Yeah she was basically my sex slave! Yeah, I dogged that pussy with this thirteen and a half inch dick. I beat them walls down! Maybe, just maybe it's a lil something left for you. Hell I didn't rape your wife! She wanted the dick, and I had no problem giving it to her."

"Styles! You shut the fuck up!"

"Nicole baby, I'm not doing a damn thang! Dr. Kareem is here in Atlanta fucking another bitch, and he can't handle the fact that someone is banging his wife. Yeah bruh, I drilled that pussy! Oh, it will be different when you hit it again."

"Y'all need to stop!"

"Fuck you Tam!"

"Cole don't talk to me like that!"

"Bitch, I will do more than talk to you! I'm gonna beat that ass!"

"No! You might hit me, but, you can't be so sure you gonna beat my ass. When you come at some ass, don't forget you got to bring some ass! Bitch don't get mad at me. Think about all those times you gave me vivid details on how Kareem was fucking you, and shortly after that, how Styles was destroying that ass! Hell, I'm a woman, and I wanted in on the action. Yeah, you were supposed to be my friend. I am your friend. That's why I wanted to keep it in the family."

"Kareem let's go."

"Okay Cole! We have a flight to catch in the morning."

"Hey brother, Mr. Styles, you get your shit. You coming with me."

"Yes ma'am, Ms. Tam."

"We have a flight to catch in the a.m. as well. So there's no need in letting this night and beautiful hotel room go to waste."

"Let's go then Ms. Tam."

After all, tomorrow is another day! We'll deal with it as it comes. Good night all!

HOT SIZZLING SEXUAL SATISFACTION

Who would have thought a super fine black solider, a stunning rich black doctor, his wife, and her friend could get caught up in a steamy, dominant, sexual romance that would later blow up like a dynamite.

Sexual Desires Unleashed!
The most refined, exclusive, and conservative *quatro* would have a sexual appetite like an animal in heat.

This book is for those who are seeking to release a prohibited sexual appetite that can no longer be contained. This book will provide you with a sexual stimulation that will spark a revolution and allow you to experience such erotic mental sex like never before.

Everyone will enjoy a new sexual encounter of a different kind! Sit back, get in a quiet private place, and let it happen.

www.ingramcontent.com/pod-product-compliance
Lightning Source LLC
LaVergne TN
LVHW091555060526
838200LV00036B/853